DOUBLE VISION

PAULINE NEVILLE

DOUBLE VISION

Saqi Books

British Library Cataloguing-in-Publication Data
A catalogue record for this book is available from the
British Library

ISBN 0 86356 360 0 (hb)

First published 2002 by Saqi Books

Saqi Books
26 Westbourne Grove
London W2 5RH
www.saqibooks.com

On the north side of the Piazza San Marco the two bronze figures on the Clock Tower hammered out the hour of eleven o'clock, and, as if in obedience to the last note, a flock of pigeons curtained to the ground. They circled the feet of the pale young woman sitting there, and she, idly dropping breadcrumbs towards their beaks, answered the older woman at her side.

'What did you say?'

'That's her. Our ship.' Audrey Martin pointed east in the direction of the lagoon. 'We're on Upper Deck.' She smiled at the crowds gathering in the square, the corners of her mouth relating to the somewhat frenzied stare in her eyes. 'I wonder which of these will be on board.'

'On board?'

'The *ship*, Aliki.'

Crumpling the croissant in her hand, Aliki spread the rest of the crumbs towards the pigeons pecking at her feet, and, wiping her hands with the napkin on her plate, let it fall into her handbag. She shifted her gaze towards the large white ship at anchor in the lagoon, and watched the birds fly.

'In flight they are one movement,' she said.

'I think I'll go and pack.' Audrey Martin stood up suddenly, the quickly glimpsed admiration around her dispelling the momentary feeling of isolation, giving impetus to her tall, self-regarding walk. Watching her move across the square Aliki ran a wet finger round the rim of the glass until she made it sing. 'One more trip is not going to make any difference,' she spoke quietly to herself.

Conscious now of heads turned in her direction, she lowered her eyes to the book on her knee. The pointed pale face, bobbed hair, boyish figure, belonged more to a youth of Renaissance Venice than to the solitary twentieth-century young woman actually sitting there.

A priest, timeless also, wearing a flat black hat – long gown sweeping the ground – hurried past, and Aliki, looking up and seeing the undulating patterns of light and shade that travelled with him, knew it was time for her to follow her mother on to the ship.

Movement continued in the Piazza, rhythmic to the central slow beat of the city, until here and there couples broke from the mass, stepped with purpose towards respective hotels where bags would be packed, bills settled and tips handed out in preparation for the water journey to the large white ship now docked beside the quay. Lifting her head to study the outline of the city, smudged now into the powder gold of the sky, Aliki flung her bag over her shoulder and said to herself: 'In the Aegean the light will be sharper.'

On board the SS *Laconia* the captain, who had recently concluded his pep talk to the crew, stood sniffing the air. Tall for a Greek, and handsome in a dark-skinned way, he was conscious of the power he wielded, not only as an emblem of mastership but also as a force in his own right. From his position on the bridge he watched embarkation from the quay and saw admiring glances cast over his ship. He was proud of the *Laconia*, knew her to be one of the most elegant ships that sailed the Ionian and Aegean seas. On shore, when dressed in civilian clothes, he sat about in tavernas listening to her praise from older men who had gone to sea. She was all white except for a discreet blue band on the funnels, and the interior was a purity of colour that, he hoped, was in the glorious tradition of Ancient Greece. Captain Manoli knew the history of the Greek people – his own, the Cretan, older still – and was almost faultless in response to the probings of his passengers. He kept his crew alert to the discerning voyagers who might seek corroboration of anything he told.

Now he descended the five decks and stood behind two

of his officers who were seated at white-clothed tables welcoming passengers on board. He listened to the multilingual voices converging into repetitive sounds of question and demand:

'Bitte ...'

'... Pardonnez-moi ...'

'... Do you think you could possibly ...?'

The English was from a tall, fair young lady who was being jostled and nudged out of the way, and as she was pushed further back down the queue the captain sent her a look of amused sympathy. Aliki caught the look, and, watching the captain turn from the jostling scene, thought of the pleasurable isolation of life on the bridge.

'Ouch!' She had trodden on the toe of the person immediately behind, and with a feeling both of surprise and apprehension heard a voice say, 'Don't mind me.' She turned to look into the face of a florid, tweedily dressed Englishman who was beaming a sort of condescending benevolence at what he considered to be a tiresome foreigner. 'Sorry,' Aliki said, and the Englishman's expression of surprise was lost in the sudden forward surge of the queue. Ahead of her Aliki could see that Audrey was already in the hands of a cabin steward, who was leading her up a stairway to the higher luxury of this one-class liner. Here amidships, in the heavily panelled main entrance, it was only the white uniformed officers who gave an indication that this was, in fact, a vessel with its hull in the water and not the foyer of a first-class hotel.

'Good evening. Welcome aboard.' The English from this square-faced officer was good, if the manner distant.

'Good evening. I wonder if my mother and I could have a table in the dining room, well ... perhaps to ourselves.' Audrey would be annoyed, but for the moment she was looking into the cool, calculating gaze of the chief purser, who said, 'And your mother's name is?'

'Audrey Martin, Mrs Martin. And my name is Aliki Findlay.' The chief purser nodded without speaking, and Aliki guessed that they would not be given a table to themselves. The officer wrote something on his table plan, and indicated that Aliki should move on. Collecting her papers inside her bag, she gratefully accepted the beaming assistance of the cabin steward now by her side. If for nothing else she would remember him for the pungent, sweat-ingrained clothing smell. His arm circled the air, half in salute, half in embrace, and his small fat frame, moving over paddling feet, led her down a passageway on the same deck. She noticed that they were not following her mother up the inner stairway. They went along the thickly carpeted passageway that seemed to take them further and further from the sea. The steward, turning twice, his grin showing a mouthful of black teeth, hurried on.

Inside the cabin, which was shaped like a capital L, Aliki went quickly to the porthole, then, turning, felt the spring in the mattress.

'Very good,' the steward informed her and, pushing a stray piece of Kleenex under the bed, turned and pointed to the button on his chest: 'Nikos is the name. I look after you strong. You have good voyage.' Sweeping a bright yellow duster across the top of the dressing-table, he pivoted through the door.

Peace at last.

Aliki sat on the bed. How long before the telephone rang? She considered the proportions of the cabin and wondered if she could put Audrey's wishes into the bend in the L in the cabin. Stretching out on the bed and ignoring the closed suitcase, she switched off the radio, which had been piping monotonous Greek music, and instead listened to the voices carrying faintly from the cabin aft, which were giving out more in the way of music than the twangings from the radio.

Italian, she thought.

Her eye fixed on the fresco above the dressing-table, and she thought she saw something move. Silver dolphins swam in an indigo sea and lotus blossoms plunged amongst a scene of spiralling leaves. Butterflies landed on leaves of eucalyptus swollen with the warmth of the sun. Her eyes shut finally and the scene shaped in behind her eyelids

The telephone shrieked in her ear.

'Hello.'

'What's happened? Where are you?'

'I'm on A Deck.'

'But how could they mix …?'

'… With three hundred on board anything could happen.'

'But darling, the fun of cabins next to each other.'

'I'll see what I can do.' Aliki ran a hand over her forehead.

'Oh do, darling.' Audrey's voice was now gently persuasive. She added, 'I've found one of the bars. Meet me in the Verandah Deck lounge in an hour.'

Aliki snapped open her case, pulled out a 'shirtwaister' and pressed the bell marked 'steward'.

'Oh, Nikos!' He had appeared almost immediately in the doorway. 'Can you bring me some ice and soda water please?' She opened the bottle of whisky bought at the airport, and, sitting at the end of the bed, poured some into a glass. Just how many of the passengers would Audrey have collected round her by the time she got to the bar?

Inside the shower she bent her head to let the spray run over her hair, down her front and back and on to the curtain at her side. She wouldn't worry about Nikos; the sight of women undressed would be nothing new to him.

By the time she emerged from the shower Nikos had been and gone. Seated in front of the dressing-table mirror she worked a hair dryer over her hair, settling the strands into her neck. She brushed and blew and let the gentle stream of air travel down her spine, and then, standing tall in front of the long mirror, Aliki slipped into the casual dress. She hoped Audrey would never find out that she was responsible for the changed cabin. It was enough that they were to be at the dining table together day following day. In the cabin she would lead her own life.

The captain, now back on the bridge, returned the salute of the officer of the watch, who had come to find the exact time of sailing.

'Twenty-two hundred hours,' the captain told the bright-eyed young Greek, who in his turn passed the information to starboard watch.

'The purser would like a word, sir.' The officer of the watch stood aside as a small, powerfully built man moved from the shadow into the light.

George Kondomanolio – a fellow Cretan – was Captain Manoli's oldest associate on the ship. He was as much the front man as any in the ship's company, having most to do with the passengers, and knowing their pleasures as well as their complaints.

'Well, Chief,' the captain addressed him, 'what's the list like this time?' He spoke in their local dialect, using words sometimes as a code between them – the texture of it abrasive and forceful – and the stocky man with the bluntly carved, tough face answered in the speech of their mother tongue:

'One chancellor of a German university, one oil tycoon, and a very beautiful ...'

'...Elena?'

'Yes.'

Captain Manoli looked towards the sun, nodded once, made a comment under his breath in which the name Apollo could just be heard and, addressing his officer once more, said, 'I've already spoken to one passenger, a young English-woman.' He liked the English passengers because they were usually modest in their demands. 'Are there many English?'

'Enough to form a queue.'

The two men exchanged looks, laughed and gave a shrug of the shoulders and a lift of their hands. They understood each other and most of those who travelled with them very well.

Alone again, the captain crossed to the other side of the bridge, looked out into the bay of Venice, once more up to the sky and saw that the little flock of high white clouds, almost static now, augured well for the evening's departure. His eyes rested on San Giorgio Maggiore on its island, enhanced now by the thick texture of light behind, and smiled once more in the direction of Apollo, whose existence he denied but whose good grace he invoked always. Beneath him now, the captain felt the first reassuring throb and vibration of the engines, precursor to any voyage – the actual moment of departure still hastening the blood circulation through his system. A ship, he had long since decided, was the supreme mistress: capricious, demanding, beautiful and above all obedient to the word of command. He had never taken a wife and now most probably never would; he was older than his suntanned healthy exterior told, and he was acquainted with most of the traumas that could, and did, happen between people. Single, he was able to devote more of his time to the fluctuating fortunes of those on his ship because he knew that, surely as calm followed storm, the reasons for argument were seldom what they seemed. In other words, people were rarely rowing about what was really eating into them.

Upstairs in the Verandah Deck lounge bar, many of the passengers had gathered to drink and view each other, and Audrey Martin, sitting in a prominent position in the middle of the room, was eyeing them over the rim of her glass and listening to snatches of conversation. Talk for the moment was about the voyage, which was to be a journey of rediscovery of the past yet from a viewpoint firmly placed in the twentieth century. Enthusiasts would be able to argue the finer points of Greek history, perhaps as seen by Professor Schliemann or the English Sir Arthur Evans, and the less enthusiastic could compare goods and prices from one bazaar to another; yet others, Aliki considered, as she walked into the bar and had a furtive look round, would see it as another way of relieving the routine of life at home. All, Aliki told herself, would have money, otherwise they wouldn't be on such a ship. She sat at the table near Audrey, and raised her eyebrows in the direction of the barman. Had she, she wondered, given enough thought to all the offerings that came from Audrey?

The champagne cocktail that sat on the table beside Mrs Martin was the result of a gesture by one of the ship's officers. First into the lounge, he had recognised the party look in the good-looking woman's eyes and had known instinctively that she would act as a magnet in such a place. He also considered that such glamour in an ageing woman deserved its own celebration. He had introduced her to Costas, the bar steward, who, because of the skill of his chosen trade, was, among all the other stewards on board, known as barman. Costas had considered the lady with the softly draped silk scarf as one to be given special treatment and had placed his favourite bowl of nuts on the table beside her. Smiling down on her with the air of a host in a country house who has just opened up his library for private viewing, he lifted the bowl towards her. Aliki, studying the champagne glass on the table, saw reflected in it the soft light of the bar and the golden dress Audrey had put on for the first evening on board. Her mother, she realised, looked very seductive. Watching now the party smile developing on Audrey's face, Aliki hoped that before long there would be someone to receive it. She lifted the glass of vodka and tonic off the tray Costas was holding at her left shoulder, and, stretching the glass towards her mother, said, 'Have a good trip.' Audrey smiled and, twisting another cigarette into her holder with an air of well-practised defiance, accepted a light from a hovering passenger and smiled broadly into the crinkled expression of an elderly man.

'Do you mind if we sit at your table?' His arm embraced the slight, ageing woman by his side.

Audrey Martin placed a hand on top of her carefully darkened hair, and then stretched out both arms to the adjoining chairs. 'This is my daughter, Aliki Findlay, and I am Audrey Martin.' The elderly couple bent forward. 'Professor and Mrs Friebel,' they said in unison. The professor handed his wife into the chair and then, sliding his right foot out in front of him, dropped into the other chair. Frau Friebel, holding on to her gentle enquiring smile, said:

'We are just coming from a tour of the United States. Now we look forward to a journey from the New World to the Old. My husband is pleased once more to visit Mount Athos.' Her husband, she told them, was a chancellor of a university in Bavaria. 'After the bustle of campus life, he is looking forward to spending a day in the calm, exclusive, male atmosphere of the sacred peninsula.' Frau Friebel laughed, the lines on her crinkled face stretching outwards.

'I believe even the animals have to be male.' Professor Friebel turned towards Aliki, and Aliki, deciding immediately that the professor and his wife would not be an intrusion on board, countered with, 'How do the generations continue?' The professor smiled, leaving the question unanswered, and Aliki watched as he shifted the position of his leg. As pain flitted across his face, she turned from it, her eyes now on a threesome making their way towards their table. The man, she thought, was from the queue earlier this evening.

'Monasteries are the main feature of the peninsula,' the professor was saying, and Aliki, still watching the three passengers, heard her mother say, 'Definitely English.'

The man in the threesome was noticeably balding, the remaining few strands of hair counted and stretched. He was of medium height and his clothes smacked of Savile Row. He had a bustling walk, and his attitude was proprietary towards the women at his side. The faces of the women told the story of much exposure to the sun; they looked healthy and well satisfied with their lot.

With any luck they will not sit here, thought Aliki, hiding behind the large menu.

'My husband takes only the senior students in Classics.' Frau Friebel was well launched into her subject. 'His energy,' she explained, 'is preserved for the exacting task of administration.'

'We are preferring a walking holiday,' Professor Friebel pointed to his outstretched leg, 'but those days are finished.' Aliki wondered if all German academics were so generous with information about themselves, and Audrey Martin, removing the cigarette stub from its holder, offered, 'Aliki's grandmother was Greek. She is called after her.'

Costas slid towards their table, carrying a tray well above his head in order to avoid other passengers coming into the room, and put two glasses of wine on the table in front of the professor.

'Have you ever tasted the Greek retsina?' Professor Friebel addressed Mrs Martin. 'When we visit the little ports on the islands we'll find a taverna and enjoy the Greek nectar.' Audrey nodded and cast an eye in the direction of the English threesome who had found a table near to them. Aliki had sunk lower in her seat.

The Englishman had his arm in the air: 'I say, George, could we …?'

'The name is Costas,' Aliki said from behind the menu.

But the words were lost in a chorus of voices heard coming through the doorway of the lounge, the owners of the voices making straight for the bar. All viewing them felt comforted that there were some Greeks travelling on this Greek ship. Up until now voices had been subdued, partly out of respect for the awe of the occasion, but now a feeling of liberation took over as warm greetings were exchanged with the bar steward, and conversations that had begun before the Greek passengers entered the room now took a firmer hold on laughter, and vibrations in the lounge were in accord with the vibrations beneath.

'Is it possible,' Audrey Martin leaned forward, 'that some people make a habit of coming on this particular cruise?'

'Some people just like cruises.' The dark-haired, coiffed woman on the Englishman's right spoke across the divide between the two tables, bringing the seated passengers closer.

The Englishman made another attempt to attract the barman, standing this time and addressing the room. 'We'll never make ourselves heard above this lot.' Over the top of the menu Aliki saw the two women turn towards each other and exchange a look that combined understanding with exasperation. She wondered if the three might be brother-in-law, wife and sister. The women, though physically different and different again from the man, resembled each other in an expression of animated anticipation. The dark, angular good looks of one and the fair, angular good looks of the other seemed in happy accord with the fleshy appearance of the man. Perhaps after all she should encourage contact with these people to keep Audrey happy on this cruise. The blood tie between her and her mother was no indication of the distance of their relationship. She looked round the large, ornate room, where mirrors on the walls helped not only to enlarge it further but to reflect the air of comfortable well-being that was beginning to take hold.

The ship's bulletin, a piece of paper slipped under each cabin door earlier in the evening, had informed passengers that tonight dress would be informal and places in the dining-room optional. The seating arrangement would not be put into effect until the following day at lunchtime. Aliki guessed that there would be studied attention to the right garment worn by each passenger, and she was surprisingly interested in what attire the Englishman would sport for the first parade.

Glasses now empty, movement out of the bar lounge began, and Aliki found herself drifting with strangers through the door, their attitude to her, as hers to them, politely friendly.

Smiles greeted them from the dining-room stewards, who, with napkins waving, saw the various passengers into their seats.

At a round table for eight, near the centre of the large room set in the middle of A Deck and far removed, it seemed, from a view of the sea, Aliki reluctantly made her way to Audrey seated in a commanding position at it. Perhaps tomorrow the purser would have managed a table for two. This time Aliki studied the menu, a huge essay on every sort of dish. She looked up and examined the room. Elderly women with neatly cut grey hair sat together nervously eyeing the ship's officers coming into the room. Healthy Scandinavians strode across the room towards what might be a window, and bright-eyed tanned playboys eased their female companions-for-the-voyage to selective seats. Aliki was pleased to see one or two – she guessed, American – academics with books in their hands.

On the whole clothes were casual but designer cut. What she really needed at that moment was some sign that this hotel – she meant ship – was about to sail. Gradually, the pale-coloured mock-pine panelling was starting to take on a richer hue as light, seen now through the door leading to the main deck deepened and then mellowed under the many small lights. The curiously sensual effect of daytime Venice was still with those sitting at the tables, and the shimmering mood of richness took over from the melancholia that had come from within the memory of a composite of marble, brick and mosaic. Aliki felt a change in herself as day tipped over into night, and was conscious of an unusual and gently enveloping feeling of curiosity.

Several dining-room stewards were circling the room with steaming dishes, and the group at the most central table – now swollen by an earnest-looking German family of four and a severe-looking American-speaking woman with a young female companion – began to bend their heads towards their plates.

As the smell of food eventually titillated her distracted senses, Aliki ate.

A hush took hold of the room and Aliki put down her knife and fork as her eyes were drawn towards the starboard exit. A large, powerful-looking man had come into the room, was assessing the tables, and was now turned towards a golden-coloured woman who seemed to radiate through her smile a warmth for all the room. Disarmed, Aliki found herself respond to both strangers in the doorway.

At ten o'clock the following morning, when the ship was well into the Adriatic, the captain held a meeting in the main lounge and introduced the passengers to such officers as were not concerned with watch-keeping duties. The officers were in their best white tropicals, the crispness of the uniforms standing out amongst the bright colours worn by the passengers. The captain spoke first in English, then French, German and Greek, giving the name of each officer and their function on the ship: 'And this is Mr Manalokas, the chief engineer, without whom we would not now be at sea.' He paused, waited while the chief stood up, gave a nod of the head and sat down. He had hardly looked at the passengers. 'And here we have the chief purser, Mr Kondomanolio, someone who will be arbitrator in all your problems.' The captain gave an encouraging laugh, which the ship's officers took up in a faint rumble across the room, the passengers following suit.

Chief Purser Kondomanolio, who was standing next to the captain with almost the same stance, remembered his brief words with him on the bridge the previous evening and merely smiled routinely at the display of faces around him. He was too old a hand to consider this batch to be any different from the last. He was, however, concerned with the passengers' well-being while on board, mainly because he sought the approval of his Cretan colleague, Captain Manoli. Belonging to a very, very ancient culture himself, he had become impervious to Greece's ancient and classical sights.

Seated on the arm of a chair a couple of feet away, Aliki glanced up at the expression that passed between the two men, and in spite of the faint air of cynicism that prevailed, she felt herself to be safe.

She sat into the chair, studied the room and saw that already small groups were forming – molecules finding their own kind. Close to the starboard exit the batch of German passengers from the dining-table the night before were laughing ponderously and the captain, who had moved amongst them and made a joke in their own tongue, now wiped his lips with a clean white handkerchief as if to expunge the taste of it from his lips. It was accepted that on these cruises into antiquity the Germans were not only the most ubiquitous but also the most discerning with their questions. Was she relieved that Professor and Frau Friebel were not grouped with them?

'They say there are about three hundred on board.' The voice came from the chair on her right and, turning, Aliki saw that one of the English 'wives' was speaking directly to her. She was a kind of honey-coloured specimen of English identity: the muted beige clothing reflecting the colour of her skin and hair, her small mouth opening and shutting like a landed fish. Beside her, in a chair pulled close, the other 'wife', dressed brilliantly from scarlet scarf to orange and white blouse, trailed her hand along the arm of the chair. Such colours would be an invitation for fusion with the sharp light in the Aegean, Aliki thought.

'Molly Wainwright,' the beige woman was saying, 'and this is my friend Daphne Miller. Peter's wife,' she added as an afterthought. 'Extraordinary how one always manages to meet one's own kind wherever one goes.'

Aliki wondered how soon she could escape from the two women, not only now but for the rest of the cruise. If Audrey spotted them across the room there would be further introductions and then no escape. She eased from behind the chair but Daphne Miller's red-tipped hand detained her. 'You must meet my husband, who is at present tucked into one of the small lounges playing backgammon with an Italian countess.'

'Yes, well … I …' Aliki had seen her mother coming across the room, her steps light, her arm held out ready for introductions. 'How lovely …' Audrey Martin began, and Daphne Miller, rising, introduced both herself and Molly Wainwright. She offered the newcomer her chair and Audrey Martin, disguising her age, shook her head.

'I was telling your – your daughter, isn't it? – that my husband is locked in battle with an Italian countess. Peter likes to feel himself at home wherever he goes.' The round, almost innocent eyes gave an impression of amused tolerance.

'What fun.' Audrey Martin's smile stretched. 'Is she with the large man with an American accent?'

'Yes. An oil tycoon, I believe.'

She's done her homework well in such a short space of time, Aliki thought, and moved slowly out of the room.

One hour later the passengers stood on deck ready for lifeboat drill. Aliki was in the third row of her group on the Sun Deck, facing a young and erect ship's officer, who had been moving up and down the lines testing and tightening lifejackets, and in some instances offering a friendly rebuke, but now, spotting his captain approaching at a smart pace down the deck, flanked by two ratings, stiffened for salute. One glance at the expression on the face of their captain told all present that the social smiling man of an hour before had been replaced by the master of the ship. He spoke in four languages, sounding a warning that on every occasion the practice bell must be obeyed. He advised them once again to become familiar with both the route to their assembly point and the putting on of the lifejacket: 'If there is a fire,' he said, 'there will be no time for mistakes.' Under the sharp eye of the captain there followed a demonstration of the lowering of lifeboats, and the crew, who had appeared from below deck, were silent and efficient under the stern scrutiny. Captain Manoli and his small contingent marched to the next assembly point and stood directly in front of the good-looking woman in the second row. Aliki watched Audrey, sensing her humiliation as the captain himself adjusted the lifejacket, turning it from back to front.

'Are you a Britisher?'

Aliki looked up from the untying of her lifejacket as a hand brushed with a thin layer of red hair reached out to help. The large man who was suddenly blocking out the light pointed to the width of his chest and gave an apologetic grin: 'Ah guess Ah'd just have to drown.'

'Oh! I hope not!' She liked the crooked grin.

Boat drill over for the day, the passengers dispersed, and Aliki, finding she was alone with the hovering American, accepted his help.

'You Britishers always like to travel on your own.' He neatly folded her lifejacket. He was from Texas, he said, caressing words out of his mouth as if he had all the time in the world.

'On our own?'

'You and the elegant lady with you will have chosen a dining table to yourselves.'

'Well ... we ... er ...'

'Ah guessed as much. Ah've been on cruises with your people before.'

'Really it's not like that. It's just that ...'

'That's fine, as Ah I love to be with people. To talk. And to eat,' he added, the smile sliding up his face again. He patted his stomach, and she remembered, of course, that she'd been at his table for breakfast. She had come into the room in a loose towelling dress slung over her bathing suit and had been asked by the chief steward not to appear like that again at meals, and had sat at the table with this American, his large frame bulging on either side of the chair, his mouth full of fish.

Now he held out his hand for introduction, and she, taking it in hers, felt both the warmth of the gesture and the strength of the hand.

'Carl Roberts,' he was saying, 'and the lady travelling with me is Maria Christina d'Capatorre, known as Elena.'

Of course, the compelling woman of the night before. A vision in a doorway and not seen by her since.

'She's at present playing backgammon with a Major Miller, found in the casino last night. She'll take the hide off him.' He laughed, and Aliki, joining in, said, 'My name is Aliki Findlay.' He tried it slowly, and said, 'You'll be Greek.'

'No. Only partly. My grandmother was.'

Maria Christina d'Capatorre, known as Elena, came up the companionway. She wore a loose kaftan, her fair hair was knotted casually on top of her head, and her face, except for the eyes, was free of make-up. Warmth radiated from her body as she undulated towards the pool. Dipping a toe into the water, she let the kaftan drop. Beneath her own towelling dress, Aliki felt herself to be cold and white. Elena's two-piece bathing suit was a flash of blue, her eyes reflecting the colour of it. Pointing her arms in the direction of the pool, she gave a jump and sped like an arrow into the water, her body hardly ruffling the surface. Carl Roberts said, 'Elena takes fine care of her body.' He grinned and, patting his stomach again, added, 'She despairs of me.' This time he gave a laugh from the stomach, the lips parting only slightly, the sound echoing back down the folds of his fat. 'I think she likes the image of beauty and the beast. Besahdes,' he added, 'Ah pay the bills.'

On a deck several beneath the Sun Deck where boat drill had taken place, the ship's doctor was taking his first clinic of the voyage, and spinning out conversation with his nervous patient in order to practise his English. He talked in a high staccato voice, announcing to all who might be passing that the surgery was open most of the twenty-four hours of the day. And Aliki, who had found her way down to this apparent dungeon, stopped in the doorway when she saw the half-naked figure lying on the couch.

'Please to come in,' the doctor said with a gesture reminiscent of a host greeting an expected guest, and Aliki, stepping forward, saw that the partly naked man lying there was Major Miller, whom she had met in the bar lounge the night before.

'It's only something for my very fair skin,' she said apologetically, and the doctor answered, 'Please to feel at home.'

Sniffing the air like a tracker dog finding its prey, Aliki

wondered if she was getting the slight fumes of alcohol or the sweet, faintly narcotic fumes of anaesthetic. 'It's only a major upset,' the doctor was saying with a confident grin, and the patient, whose stomach had given him cramps through the night, said, 'I think you mean *minor* upset.' The Major, Aliki decided, had not understood the doctor's joke. She watched as the doctor, in small, neat handwriting, wrote on the side of a bottle, 'Twice daily after meals,' and then, standing, which meant the top of his head levelled with Peter Miller's neck, stuck out his hand and said, 'No need to come again.'

Peter Miller shook his hand, looked down into a pair of quietly discerning eyes and felt a new reassurance. He walked quickly out of the dark cabin that was used as a sick bay, avoiding the eyes of the attractive young woman standing there, moved towards the stairway that took him four flights to Upper Deck, along to the passageway to the cabin next to his and Daphne's, and without knocking opened the door.

Molly Wainwright was just stepping into a bathing suit when Peter Miller walked in. 'Take a seat,', she said, clearing some clothes, and watched as he flopped into a chair.

'I've just seen the doctor about my stomach. Funny man. Possibly sees himself as something of a philosopher.' He turned in his chair to examine Molly's figure. It would not be the best on board but it could serve as a guide to other middle-aged woman who mistakenly fancied themselves in a two-piece bathing suit. Molly stood still, allowing the inspection, while Peter, studying the muted effect, said, 'I wish

Daphne could be a bit more subtle in her colours. Well, old girl,' he said, giving the rump in front of him a fair whack, 'let's go and view the rest of the talent on board.'

There was a knock on the door and the fat stewardess of Upper Deck came in with a bucket and cleaning materials. 'I do cabin now.'

She found the English passengers, with their attention to detail and slow habits in the morning, irritating. When others were up on deck having drinks, sunbathing or swimming, the English would still be in their cabin asking to iron their own clothes or ordering cups of tea.

Peter Miller, ignoring the stewardess who had slipped between him and the bathroom, lifted the large bag containing sun oils, books, magazines and boxes of Kleenex, and with an arm round Molly's shoulder moved them both through the door. The stewardess watched and wondered who it was who actually slept in this cabin.

On the way to the Verandah Deck Peter Miller and Molly Wainwright ran into the sophisticated-looking Englishwoman and the pale silent daughter. Molly introduced Peter to them, and he unhesitatingly said, 'Join us on deck for a glass of ouzo.' He addressed himself to the older woman but turned now to look at the younger. 'That would be nice,' Audrey Martin said, and, without consulting Aliki, turned with him to walk up the stairway. Aliki followed, her fears now a certainty that this was to be the nucleus of the group her mother – and probably the Millers – would form.

'Are you going ashore at our first port of call? Corfu, I believe.'

Aliki found that she was in step with the beige woman who had spoken to her earlier – a part of the Miller group. She said, 'No. I think I'll … stay on board.' The slow speed of the ship and avoidance of land while the passengers became acquainted seemed as contrived as were the welcoming good manners of the bored ship's officers.

'But Corfu is so lovely.'

'It's the Aegean islands I've come to see,' Aliki explained. 'I'm interested in the Cretan early culture. The Minoan.' She registered the surprised look on the other woman's face. And, turning, she walked briskly towards a shaded part of the deck, sensing the calculating look from behind. Flopping into a deck chair near the rails, she looked with an excluding concentration at the movement of the sea.

All around the perimeter of the deck, about three yards from the pool, deck chairs had been opened by stewards and were acting now as an invitation to those coming on deck. Tables were scattered here and there under coloured umbrellas, and already passengers in sportswear were sitting under them. Out of the corner of her eye Aliki could see that Daphne Miller – her face almost unrecognisable behind a pair of bright orange sunglasses, her skin wet from a combination of oil and sweat – had raised herself out of the deck chair. 'Do all have a seat,' she said, pointing to some empty chairs, and the tone of her voice and the words spoken reminded Aliki of afternoons spent with the great aunts in their flat off Kensington High Street.

Sinking further into her chair and opening her book on

the history of Crete, she looked at the pictures of some of the beautiful, small Ancient Cretan women, hair ornately dressed and erect, and, peering closely, saw from the pictures that topless dresses – skirts long – were fashionable a very long time ago. She cast a glance at the semi-bronzed figures lying on the deck around her and wondered what Antiquity would make of style today. The pleasant feeling of anonymity that had accompanied her on to the ship and into the secretly arranged cabin was beginning to evaporate, until a honeyed voice at her elbow said, 'It is beautiful.' Elena was lying near her on the deck.

'Yes. Lovely. But too hot for me.' She felt prim and out of place, and, seeing the small freckles appearing on her body, disliked what she saw. Wasn't it Arthur who had said freckles turned him on? What else did she remember? It can't only have been the sweet rotting smell of gin? She stared ahead of her and thought how she had married him as a form of escape from the lifestyle with her mother, but found she had moved from one tyranny to another: the tyranny of Arthur's dedication, then addiction, to drink. At first the bottle of wine every night had added to dinner. But even on the honeymoon, where there was a certain intimacy, she had not realised that the bottles of skin tonic, hair lotion and aftershave were actually full of booze.

She sat up suddenly and looked through the railings at the navy-blue, bulging sea. Had she also been hoping through marriage to be clear of the family's mental disturbance? She'd found it was in her Irish grandfather; also, perhaps, in Audrey.

Oh God. How hereditary was it? Her gaze fixed on some seagulls fighting near the hold. She had thought that in a marriage to a much older man she would be free to continue her day-dreaming, fantasising journeys into books. But she tried now to look it straight in the face: had she ever given it proper thought? Her journeys into books had brought her to the Minoan period, three thousand years ago, with their Earth Mother and their oneness with nature.

The seagulls had risen straight up into the air like helicopters from a launch pad, her thoughts going with them.

From the deck came, 'What are you thinking about?' Elena was stretching and rising to her feet.

'Birds,' Aliki said, still watching the gliding movements. But, closing her book, she pulled her chair into the shade of two lifeboats that were interrupting the scorching rays of the sun.

A plop into the sea, and she was up again peering through the rails. A bucket was being drawn into the hold and, following its progress with her eyes, Aliki thought for a moment of the men who worked and lived down there.

She leaned on the rails and looked starboard. As far as the eye could see, water moved on in stretches of green-blue undulating silk. Aliki lifted her head and breathed in the clear air around her.

Forward, two white-coated stewards were spreading cloths on long tables, and, as if in answer to this silent summons, Peter Miller put his arm in the air. 'Another drink, anyone?'

'I think we've had enough for now, Peter.' Daphne Miller

rose and, rubbing blobs of sweat and oil back into her skin, said, 'What about some lunch?'

Stretching out an arm to lift Elena from the deck and moving with her towards the table, Carl Roberts pointed to a display of stuffed vine leaves, black and green olives in oil, pancakes, feta cheese and honey and almond cakes, and, calling for the steward, ordered two bottles of retsina.

Aliki, who had moved towards the table, had watched the dance-like movements of Carl Roberts's surprisingly small feet and once again thought how she had seen this before in large people. Was there something attractive about this paradox of grace and size?

Greek music was coming through the loudspeakers and above them, seagulls flew gracefully as if in time to it. A pleasant, faintly scented breeze seemed to caress the ship and reach the bridge, where the captain, who was standing out on one of the wings, was giving silent thanks to the god he consulted – but of course did not believe in – that the atmosphere in his ship was apparently untroubled. Watching the serving of food on to plates, he considered how meal time was always a period of calm, and very often the sleep that followed it gave some of his officers and stewards a breathing space. He smiled to himself when he thought of the transformation that took place when members of his crew went ashore in civilian clothes, passengers passing them as strangers, not realising that the relaxed man in a T-shirt was the same person they had seen as a formal ship's officer in a crisp white uniform. One of the instructions he always had to give to new recruits was to learn at what point their accepted good manners when dealing with passengers should turn into restraint. Further – and here the captain drew in his breath – they were not to believe all the flattery that came their way.

Turning now to the chief purser, who had considered matters stable enough to leave his office, the captain said, 'Well, Chief, what do you think of this batch?' The chief purser, looking over the rail at the scorching bodies below, said, 'The doctor will have a patient or two in the sick bay tomorrow.'

The captain gripped the rail. 'Sunburn the doctor can cope with, but sunstroke we cannot allow.' He stood tall. 'Go on deck and issue them all with hats.'

'This is not a military ship, sir, and we don't hand out issue.'

'Well, then,' the captain commanded, 'tell the deck stewards to tell the cabin steward to bring hats from the cabins. It seems we've got a bunch of unseasoned travellers on board.'

'Sir.' The chief purser moved to speak through the intercom. Turning to his captain, he said, 'You know, sir, we've got Mr Roberts on board.'

'He's already been into my office.'

'Ah.' The chief purser saluted and turned on his heel.

Lunch over for those on the Sun Deck, afternoon gradually drowsed into evening, and the deck became a patchwork of interesting garments as passengers came to observe sunset at sea. Occasionally the clink of glass could be heard, and those more interested in the casinos than in watching the descending sun had gone below, preparing to be first into the dining-room for the first sitting and the first to the gambling tables where chips and the green baize awaited them. Others would be dressing for the second sitting and the long slow discovery through the dinner menu of what they were going to eat, while others would be in the bar well on their way to a bad hangover the following day.

Later that night, following a full day in the clear air, Aliki had expected to drop quickly into sleep, but high-pitched voices were disturbing her. She listened carefully. Was she perhaps, like Gilbert Pinfold, hearing them in her head? But the voices continued.

She switched on the light and climbed out of bed. 'Why should I go on?' a young female voice questioned, and the answer, 'But you agreed to come on this trip,' seemed a sensible one to Aliki. Could the voices belong to the Canadian couple – perhaps mother and daughter, perhaps teacher and pupil, perhaps woman with young lover – who had sat silently at their table on the first night? In the morning she would go to the purser's office and complain that the partition between the two cabins was not strong enough. Now that she studied the locked door, she could see there was a thread of light all round the perimeter.

The voices continued and, crossing the floor, Aliki put her ear against the wall. The tones had lowered. She was almost certain they came from the severe, dominant woman and the frightened girl. From the cabin on the other side there was only the silence of deep, contented sleep. She ran her toes over the thick carpet, wondering whether if she rang the bell at this hour Nikos would appear. He had been outside her cabin when she'd come to bed, asking if there was anything to press. He seemed to invite work; the sweat of the man, the sweet-sour smell lingered on in the dress he pressed for her every evening.

'Tonight you wear another dress,' he had said, removing the used glasses from her room, and Aliki, who was amused by his proprietorial air, said, 'Oh, you think so, do you?'

Now she sat on the bench under the porthole and looked at the night sky. Tiny jewels of light punctured the darkness; otherwise there was nothing out there to disturb the habits of the creatures of the night. Inside the ship there would be crumpled beds, dreams, hot pillows, mild indigestion, and, in some instances, somewhat heaving love-making and, yes, arguments. She turned back to face the cabin and found that the distant swell of water was a consolation in the gripping silence that was now around her. She paced the floor and looked once more towards the porthole. Here, at the point where today was becoming tomorrow, she had the familiar feeling of suspension. She touched the bed, the pillows, her pyjamas, her hair brush and, unzipping her bag, took out a bottle of sleeping pills. Unscrewing the bottle top, she hesitated, looking at the ones in her hand, and then tipped them all into the basin and ran the taps.

The voices in the cabin aft had begun again. The note of appeal had been replaced by one of anger:

'I can do what I like with my life.'

'But Tessa ...'

Tears now, and Aliki thought of her own, the silent ones when her father had been killed in a riding accident. The pain had been too deep for tears; the abandonment she felt, inexplicable: that he, the sound, adjusted member of the family, should have thrown himself and his horse at a five-bar gate on the hunting field and failed to handle the landing. She stood up and said to the empty room, 'I lost my father through bravado. He only survived the devastation of the fall for a few months. In a wheelchair,' she added.

At the time she was in boarding school, recently having been introduced to the extensive library in the main school building, and had begun her study of ancient Greece – her mother's people, she often had to remind herself. The head had sent for her and Aliki, walking into the room, had known fear when she saw her mother standing there, her face drained and solemn.

'Your father died this morning from a brain haemorrhage.' Audrey spoke in a monotone, but the voice was pleading. The news meant nothing to Aliki at first because she couldn't take it in. Wouldn't take it in. Then it came to her that she was to take over as the parent/companion to her mother and that for an indefinite period they would be alone together.

The head had tried to argue against Audrey's plan to take Aliki out of school then. But Audrey had prevailed, and in a sleepwalk Aliki had packed her bags, feeling she had lost her life along with her father's.

They visited her grandfather in County Wexford from time to time, and she found that it was only when she and he were in his library together that they could communicate. She had not really understood his hesitation about almost everything, so had stuck to the subject of books. He gave her a good grounding. She felt she could have loved that old man if he had let her close enough.

Her cousins were mostly absorbed with superstition and fortune-telling, so it was no surprise when the elder ones suggested she visit May Morgan. 'She's the best fortune-teller in Ireland and will tell you what to do.'

'To do?'

'How to get away from your mother.'

She had gone to the small thatched cottage, with barking dogs and two black cats to guard it, and, seeing the bent elderly woman in the doorway, couldn't believe that anyone could look so like a witch and not be one.

'Come away in, girl dear,' the old crone cackled, 'and sit opposite me.'

She held out her hand and felt the electric touch of the parched skin. She jumped back when the witch said, 'Did ever you see the like?'

'What?' Aliki cried out.

''Tis ruled by fate ye're,' May Morgan said, pushing her

hand away. 'I can do nothing for you.'

She had not waited to hear anything more, had crept out of the cottage past growling dogs and hissing cats, swearing never to return and knowing she had received not a death sentence but a life sentence against the operating of her own will.

The tears that could not come for her father flowed now as she realised that fate had singled her out. The maids in the rambling old house had sensed something strange about her and were temporarily afraid. She had gone to her room, locked the door, had looked at herself in the mirror and had seen fear and entrapment. Staring long, she knew the moment had come to make a decision but instead she said to her own reflection, 'All right. If that's the way of it. All right.'

She'd fallen in with Audrey's plans, and the first was a school-leaving present of a world tour, at the end of which Audrey's address book was full of telephone numbers of – what she hoped would be – gentleman callers for Aliki. Possibly one of the elderly rich they had found sitting in elegant lounges in respectable hotels.

One or two called, and then never returned. Others tried to break the bond – whatever that was – between mother and daughter, but Aliki's indifference proved a further barrier. It was not that Audrey Martin was against a good match for Aliki, it was simply that she wanted a man she could mould. And then there was Arthur. He was the most persistent and the most agreeable. He liked Audrey Martin's dominating ways.

Her mother said to her, 'Darling, he's rich and reliable. What more do you want?' And Aliki knew she couldn't think what. Their courtship she had not seen as fun, but she quite liked the *habit* of Arthur. She feared her mother's enthusiasm might put him off, but Arthur, she discovered later, wanted guidance.

The wedding ceremony was as stark as the hope in her heart, and Audrey's fussing over wedding garments did nothing to stir her interest. Although Arthur was kind at first – the older man proud of his good-looking young wife – she had sensed the void, a void for which she had been partly responsible. When the novelty wore off, Arthur started to spend days away, and then nights. The vacuum was filled by Audrey who began her course of 'just dropping in.'

At first Aliki suspected Arthur was seeing another woman but soon came to realise that he was not fit enough. The remorse that came with each return home had to be deadened by alcohol. And more alcohol. In time she came to realise that alcohol was in itself the problem. At first he'd done his drinking in clubs or wine bars on his way home from the City. But soon it was alone in his study. Eventually he resented any time away from the bottle, and finally the relationship with the bottle was all there was. One day she found him dead in his bed, the bottle lying dripping on to his chest.

It was inevitable that she would move back in with her mother, who at this stage in her life had given up the drudgery of running a house and was – at least temporarily –

balanced in the luxury of a large service flat in Knightsbridge. Arthur's belongings were taken by the children from his previous marriage, and Aliki, closing the door of their almost unlived-in house, handed the keys to the eldest son.

She took with her the beautiful flower painting by the German artist, Nolde, which Arthur had given her as a wedding present, a life's interest in the estate until further marriage and her large portfolio of books. The books formed the basis of what she hoped might one day be the return of her life.

There was a violent knocking on her cabin door, and before she had time to put on her dressing-gown the girl from the next cabin was standing in the doorway, her face white, her eyes black. She was smiling grotesquely at Aliki, and saying, 'My name is Tessa. Can I stay here?' She sat on the bench under the porthole. She looked round the cabin. 'I'm dying, you know. Slowly of a blood disease.' Opening the cupboard door, Aliki took out the bottle of whisky and put it on the table.

'Have a drink. I mean, let's drink to your dying.' She stared at the slightly mad but healthy-looking girl. Tessa stood up, spun round and said, 'Don't you care?' She was grinning again. 'Not even a teeny bit?'

In fact, Aliki was wondering if she could stop herself from being sick, actually vomiting out into the room.

'Does your ...?'

'... nurse,' Tessa supplied.

'Does your nurse know you're in here?' Aliki saw that

Tessa's eyes were fixed on the wet mass of congealed sleeping pills in the basin. She said, 'I could get a sleeping pill from the night-nurse for you.'

'Sleep! I don't want to sleep. I want to be awake day and night, making the most of my time. My nurse wants me to stay in bed most of the time. That is the trouble.' She began to walk on tiptoe, her arms out like a dancer. 'I want to have fun. Meet some of the passengers, play some of the deck games.'

'I'll help you,' Aliki heard herself say.

Tessa spun round to look through the porthole, and Aliki wondered whether Tessa's companion would come if she knocked on the wall. By now she must be looking for her charge. She said, 'I think it's time you returned to your cabin ...'

'... and when we've practised we'll enter a deck quoit competition, and, and ...' Her voice was rising, pink spots appearing on the white cheeks, '... there will be a prize for the two winners.'

Aliki wondered if there might be some subtlety behind the derangement. But she said, 'Tessa, it is the middle of the night and by now your nurse must have missed you. May even be looking for you. I think it's time you returned to your cabin.' She opened the door and saw that the light was on in the passageway, and the night steward was coming towards them. Turning sideways, he brushed past Aliki and, seeing the pale excited girl, said to the English lady, 'Do you need the doctor?' Aliki hesitated, but, spotting the girl's companion coming towards them, shook her head. The companion wore a thick dressing-gown and a scarf round her neck. Her face was white and strained and the lids of her eyes fluttered nervously.

'Come now, Tessa,' she said. 'You're disturbing the whole ship.' She held out her hand, and it was the gesture Aliki had seen across the dining-table, mistaking it then for authority. 'I must apologise for this interruption to your sleep.' The woman spoke with a gentle Canadian accent in a slow, tired voice.

'I wasn't asleep. In fact, Tessa and I were discussing a game we might play.' She felt sudden sympathy for the girl.

'Game?' the tired voice questioned.

'Well, of course not now, but later. Perhaps in a few days ...' Her voice trailed.

Letting her hands drop to her sides, Tessa walked towards the door as if she were in a sleep, and seeing her like this Aliki wondered if the whole scene was a sleepwalk. Her own, perhaps? At the cabin door the girl turned round. 'Thanks,' she said. Once more the nurse apologised and, lifting the bottom of her long gown, hurried after Tessa.

Aliki walked slowly round the room, then, quickening her pace, she picked up both glasses and threw the drink into the basin. Was she awake wondering if she had been in a dream? Or asleep questioning if she were awake? Was the scene in which she'd just taken part in some way a part of her own visions? Was Tessa's distress a part of her own? She began to finger things: the door handle between the cabins, the bench where Tessa had sat and again the glasses. Yes. The girl had been here. But she didn't believe in her illness, nor that she was travelling with a nurse. The strange grey lady, in her thick dressing-gown, had offered no explanation and she had asked for none. But if anyone was sick she guessed it was the older woman. Perhaps there actually would be a moment on the voyage when Tessa might tell her the truth.

She lay on her bed and a slight warmth began to flow through her. Sleep came hesitatingly, and just before she shut her eyes there was movement in the fresco opposite. Smiling, she embraced the gentle Muse.

By the time the ship had stopped off at Corfu and most of the passengers had gone ashore to watch cricket on the 'village green', Aliki had begun to wonder if indeed she was on a Greek ship cruising through the Greek islands, acquainting herself with both modern and ancient Greece, or on some British banana boat delivering and collecting in the Caribbean. But now, with the arrival at Piraeus, the bustle and noise of a busy Greek port and the presence of Nikos pivoting round her cabin, the right atmosphere had been restored. He dusted and hummed, intermittently telling her of his visit today to his house in the outskirts of Athens, to his wife and to his five children. The hum changed to a low whistle as he accepted from his lady the Greek money to be spent on his children.

'Today you go ashore,' he commanded, and whistled his way out of the cabin.

From her position on the Sun Deck Aliki watched the crowds milling about on the quay, some making greetings, others with gestures of departure, and amongst them she saw members of the ship's crew disembarking from the hold. The short, fat figure of Nikos, dressed in dark trousers and a bright orange shirt, hurried through, his movements more like a spinning top than a householder walking through familiar streets to his home. This morning, when she had given him the drachmas to spend on his wife and family, she had at the same time mentioned the couple next door.

'Is sick,' Nikos indicated with his head, and when she'd answered that she doubted it, Nikos had given an ambiguous, 'But I know.'

Now she looked round to see if there was any sign of Tessa on deck, and came face to face with Peter Miller, who said, 'How about all sharing a taxi from Piraeus up to Athens?'

'I'm not sure that my mother is going ashore.'

'She's here now.'

Audrey appeared up the companionway, flanked by the Major's two women. She called out to Aliki, 'Let's share with the Millers.' They stood watching disembarkation.

'If the taxi ride's to be worth it we'd better go.' Peter Miller came along the deck holding out his arms as if to herd them all together.

This morning the Major was in a dark blue, open-necked shirt, neatly pressed white trousers, and, beneath these, white kid shoes. The tan that was beginning to spread over his skin was giving a voluptuous, almost Latin look to this defiantly English Englishman.

Bustling down the companionway behind his wife, he said in a voice that carried in the sharp clear air, 'If I were you, darling, I'd have some of that mop cut.' He examined his wife's recent hair-set as she turned to look at him.

'Well, you're not me, are you?' she countered, looking at her husband's few strands of hair, and exchanged smiles with Molly Wainwright following behind. The peacock blue of her silk shirt and linen trousers to match were a magnet for the sun.

Inside the taxi the five sat sardined together, sweating and breathing deeply as the driver, regarding green and red lights alike, used every pedestrian as a target.

'God, it's stifling.' Audrey Martin wound down the window and Peter Miller, leaning over her, rewound it. 'Would you prefer draughts?'

'We're not in England now,' Audrey Martin said primly. Tempers were frayed by the time they arrived in Constitution Square, and Peter Miller, backing from Audrey Martin and her daughter, linked arms with his two women and said, 'All right, then, if you don't want to join us in a hunt for a favourite restaurant we'll see you back at the ship.'

Gratefully Aliki followed her mother to a shaded café where they ordered a bottle of retsina and some honey and nut cakes.

'Thank goodness he's gone,' Aliki said.

'I like him,' Audrey said defiantly. 'He gets things going.'

Aliki leant towards her mother. 'Last night that strange Canadian girl who sat at our table on the first night came bursting into my cabin, she'd practically nothing on.'

'Aliki! Please!'

'I talked to my cabin steward about it this morning. He's going to refer it to the ship's doctor.'

'She has no business to be on board.'

'Why not?'

'It's frightening for people.' Aliki turned from her mother.

At a table near where they sat, a handsome man with a surprisingly familiar face was in animated conversation with a red-headed girl. Together they smiled towards Audrey and Aliki. 'Haven't we seen them somewhere?' Audrey's smile was hesitant.

'Yes. On the ship. It's the captain and one of the ship's hostesses.'

Audrey Martin looked at them through partly closed eyes. 'She's pretty in a way.' And Aliki, who had just spotted another familiar face among the tables, said, 'Yes she is.' In fact, she was looking at the tumbling little woman of rubber limbs who had been spin-balled from one man to another in the cabaret last night.

Audrey Martin turned in her seat. 'What is it?' Aliki asked.

'I can't help wondering if you are really enjoying yourself.'

'Of course I am.'

Audrey persisted. 'I think you could be a little more friendly to some of the passengers. What about the unattached men who notice you during the cabaret at night?'

Aliki stared at her mother.

'Soon I shall stop trying for you.' A petulant note had come into Audrey's voice, and Aliki, recognising it, said, 'I wonder what we're going to find in the shops.' She poured from the bottle of wine and munched one of the little cakes the waiter had just brought. Savouring the cake's sweet richness, she thought of the contrasting astringent thinness of the wine and wondered if, perhaps, the taste was a reflection of the masculine tone of the city.

She smiled inwardly: even the grey-eyed goddess had been the enemy of romantic sweetness. Wise in counsel, yes, and fond of her battle-origin birth. The worship of Athena had been pure, civilised, the idea of romance unknown to classical Greece.

'Aliki!' What are you thinking about?' Audrey chanced.

Aliki dared, 'About classical Greece. It's a far cry from the bustle of life today,' she said, looking at the cars hurtling past.

'I think we had better go shopping before it gets any hotter.' Audrey Martin got rapidly to her feet, and Aliki, rising slowly and moving out from the shade, felt the heat like a vice round her head.

Shopkeepers were at first surprised and then pleased by this middle-of-the-day visit from the two tall, fair-skinned women who came into their shops, not only to look but also to buy. They'd rapidly pulled up the shades and shaken themselves from their afternoon sleep.

'Good morning madam,' was what Audrey had hoped to hear, but instead it was a hard-eyed greeting and a display of what Aliki saw as a jumble of trinkets.

Audrey Martin, who was a compulsive buyer and who liked in each place she visited to acquire something in memory of it, chose on this occasion silver. They walked up and down the narrow streets, in and out of the shops, until in one Audrey came to rest. She bought a silver eternity ring, with tiny classical carvings on it, and gave it at once to Aliki. Turning to the owner of the shop, she pointed to her ears and said, 'For me, earrings.'

Trays of earrings were produced and more trays. As Audrey walked up and down in the airless small shop, examining her reflection in the various mirrors, Aliki's hand ran impatiently backwards and forwards on the glass top of the jewel case.

'These are too small,' Audrey said, shaking her head. And, 'These are not important enough. We might find something with a little more life,' she said, peering into the cases.

The shopkeeper, who was admiring the local silver hanging now from the good-looking woman's ears, said, 'It is good that the earrings fit in with the whole.' His hands caressed as it were Audrey's figure, and his smile echoed the gesture. 'That's what I mean,' Audrey said, fluffing up her hair as she peered into the mirror. Turning to face the shopkeeper, she said, 'I'll try just a couple more.'

Revolving the newly acquired ring on the third finger of her right hand and seeing the sweat beads gathering under it, Aliki said, 'Let's go back to the ship. You're never going to make up your mind.'

Audrey Martin pushed the hair behind her ears and, smiling at her reflection, said, 'I'll just look in that other tray.'

While her mother bargained and looked, and looked again and bargained, Aliki left the shop and stood under the awning outside. She supposed it was her lack of interest in possessions generally that made her restless during these protracted haggling sessions. Perhaps it was the Greek blood in Audrey that excited her into making deals. Just how many pairs of earrings would she collect for the price of one? She looked now at her own narrow, almost transparent image in the shop window and wondered if she were the sort of person who looked best against a background of moonlight, her daytime reflection more like a photograph negative.

'Come on darling.' Audrey appeared triumphantly through the shop door, her springing walk a defiance of the heat, the tiny peals of sound that come from the bell-like earrings vibrating into it. She ignored Aliki's lack of interest as they walked slowly down the hot street where the pavement seemed to give out electric sparks.

'All right,' Audrey said finally, 'let's get a taxi and return to the ship.'

Inside the taxi, Aliki rested her head against the back seat and listened to the driver shout abuse at every pedestrian who dared to cross his path. 'I wonder why they're so angry.'

'That's not anger, that's just the male bird claiming his territory.' In silence they hung on to the sides of the car as it was bumped down to the quayside, Aliki praying that Audrey would give the man the fee he asked.

Once in her cabin – now on the shaded side of the ship – Aliki let out her breath. She lay on her bed and let the cool air waft over her. With any luck, she thought, they would have shaken off the Major. Her eyes drifted towards the fresco on the wall. An evening spent with the cool Contessa – if indeed she were that – and her American friend would be nice. She pictured them now in their luxurious stateroom, her mind on the bottle of champagne that might sit between them.

But in fact Elena was lying on her back, a mud pack on her face. She had counted to one hundred in Greek and, having skimmed through the other numbers in English, was now prepared to talk.

Carl Roberts, enveloped in a large bathrobe and looking like a well-fed porpoise, continued to address Elena out of the side of his slightly crooked mouth, whilst running a hand along the length of her leg.

'What's your view of the passengers, honey? You know Ah brought you here to have fun.'

'I always have fun.'

'Ah mean, could any of them interest us?'

Elena got off the bed, slipped a white silk dressing-gown round her shoulders and ran the taps. Slowly she circled her face with damp cotton wool and removed the mask. The grey-eyed, alert face resumed its normal shade. She addressed the reflection in the basin mirror. 'The only one,' she pulled down her blonde hair and lowered her eyelids in imitation, 'is the fair English girl with the elaborate mother.'

Carl Roberts laughed at the mimicry. 'Sure. She talks to me sometimes. Seems to like my Southern drawl which Ah spin out for her.'

'But where are their men?'

Carl Roberts smiled. 'Ah like it the way it is.'

Elena began to dress by first slipping off the silk dressing-gown and immediately stepping into a clinging black dress with a plunging neckline, both she and Carl Roberts admiring the outline.

'Well, honey, Ah've been figuring out why you agreed to come on this cruise with me. It's not as if ...'

'You are my friend.' She put her arms round his neck and, reaching down, placed her cheek against his. Such friendship, he knew, was ephemeral.

Their dressing complete, the couple sat each in a white armchair, pouring from the bottle of champagne and opening the backgammon board. It was understood between them that Elena was the better player, but it was also understood that Carl did not mind this type of defeat. Competing over such small stakes was of little account; besides, he liked to see the battle light in Elena's eyes. Now as he put out the counters in preparation for the game he laughed and said,

'Ah won't forget the expression on the Englishman's face when he found out you know the game.'

'Poor Major Miller!' Elena moved her arm across the board. The Englishman with his ego-boosting front of two women was not someone to be given much consideration. Carl, for all his gross appearance and large air of benevolence, was in fact the sort of shrewd operator she could appreciate. He was a no-nonsense man, with his feet firmly on the ground of whichever property he had recently acquired. She smiled to herself as she took one of his men on the board, and watched Carl make the mistake she had planned for him. 'We might ask the English girl – without the mother – for a drink some time.'

Carl Roberts agreed: it was the small diversion he had been planning for himself. Getting through to that young woman just might have its interests.

'Yeah. We'll do that.'

The English girl was in her cabin reading the ship's bulletin

for the following day. It had just been pushed under the door, and now, following it, came Nikos.

'I finish pressing.' He held up the sea-green dress that Aliki had offered him each morning. 'Very pretty,' he said, 'but tonight you change.'

Aliki smiled to herself and handed him a day dress from her case. Nikos took hold of it and pushed it into the cupboard.

'Please, Nikos, you know it will crease in there.'

'Is good. Now out of the way.'

She could see that Nikos considered the cabins belonged to him, the passengers merely tenants of them. And the passengers on the whole put up with his proprietorial manner because in the process of owning the cabins and attending to their needs he probably created for them an atmosphere that was, as it happened, a substitute for home. Now he picked up a sparkling silver dress out of the case and said, 'Tonight you go dancing on deck. Is very pretty under the moon.'

Aliki wondered if ships had an arrangement with Selene that she shine through all the nights of a cruise. She watched as Nikos swept his yellow duster across the dressing-table, shifted the silver dress to his other arm and made for the door. He turned. 'Is not good that you keep cabin door unlocked at night.' He nodded in the direction of the cabin aft and hummed his way out of the cabin.

Aliki sat still, contemplating the door of the cabin aft, and wondered: had the nurse managed to quiet – even understand – the hysterical girl with the feigned death-wish?

Now she swung round to look at the dress hanging on the cupboard. Was her lack of interest in clothes due to her mother's interference over the years? Her father had admired her simple taste and was proud of her graceful, boyish figure, every now and again straightening her back as she walked, telling her that one was nothing unless one walked tall. But he had not lived long enough to see taste develop into style.

She sat back on the bed. Even now she couldn't forgive him for leaving her just as she was beginning to connect home feelings with the outside world, establish her own personality, learn to resist her mother. After his death her resolve collapsed, and she had given in to Audrey's mode of living. Audrey's mode was based on her need for amusement and pleasure. Pleasure, for her, was to dress up every evening in preparation for a party that might never come. On the whole Aliki hated parties: empty chatter, hot, sticky hands, insinuations, bold invitations. But, she hesitated, it had been at a party that she had found her escape: Arthur and a proposal of marriage. It seemed at first like a replacement for her father. Once married, she had thrown away most of her dresses in favour of a shirt and a pair of jeans. Now, and for the last few years, she had chosen clothes that merged with the muted personality that had become her shield.

She stood up suddenly, and listened. Raised voices were coming through the wall and the loudest seemed to belong to Nikos.

'Is wrong to cut hair. Is a sin. Now no boy will look at you.'

The door to the next cabin was open and when Aliki walked in she saw that Tessa was by the porthole, a razor in her hand, thrusting it towards Nikos. He, with his fat arm stretched, was making cooing comforting noises, and saying finally, 'If you give it here I finish cutting hair.'

Tessa, crouched now between the beds, her brush of short hair giving her the appearance of a woodland animal backing into cover, said, 'I swear I shall use the razor if you come closer.' Her eyes were bright.

Like the tongue of an adder Nikos's arm shot out from his side and locked on to the joint of Tessa's arm. The razor fell to the floor and Tessa, laughing, said, 'Okay, you cut it.' Aliki understood suddenly that attention of any sort was vital to her.

In a whisper Nikos said to Aliki, 'Soon I find empty cabin. Is better she sleep alone.' And Aliki, who was still standing by the door, grinned at Nikos, 'It is not your business, Nikos,' but she knew already that he thought it was.

'Is good idea.' The tapering continued, Nikos's tongue caught in the grip of his teeth, Tessa now placid and yielding.

Aliki looked from one to the other, seeing Nikos for the nanny figure he was, and walked out of the room.

From the passageway she turned round. 'Where is Tessa's companion?'

'Swimming. She get strong.'

Aliki took this ambiguous remark into her own cabin, where the telephone was ringing.

'Hello?'

'I'm going to play bridge this evening, and have asked to dine with the first sitting. Will you be all right?' Her mother's voice was determined.

'I'm glad you've found a four. Who are they?' She felt she should show interest.

'Molly Wainwright, Carl Roberts and some little Englishman whom Major Miller found near the Sun Deck bar drinking tea.'

'I'll probably see the film. I believe it's *High Society*.' Aliki put down the telephone. Relief flooded through her. Now her mother was launched.

Picking up the receiver once more, she dialled the ship's operator. 'Cabin A30 please.'

'Hello?' Nikos's voice answered.

'Is Tessa all right?'

'Is better. Short hair very good. Now she is getting ready for dinner. The lady has returned.'

Sitting in what had become her favourite position, by the porthole with her body twisted towards the fresco on the wall, Aliki opened her large book on the ancient Minoans and compared the figures illustrated in it with those on the wall. Here were the same erect men and women. The women with long coiled hair, billowing skirts, naked breasts, and the men in short tunics hardly covering their genitals. Was freedom of bodily expression a feature of long ago? She nodded her head. The last time she had studied the fresco it was of dolphins swimming in an indigo sea. Had the mystery of this ancient civilisation concentrated into her room? Had the love of nature so prevalent with these long, long ago people come so alive in her thinking that she was seeing what she was reading about here in front of her? Not only seeing but feeling their presence. What, she wondered, had any of this to do with her present condition? And what, indeed, was her present condition? She looked in the mirror. Could she see a sort of reawakening there? With a fleeting glance at the fresco on the wall, she saw that it had resumed its static beauty, and she began to dress slowly for dinner.

Later that night, in the cool of the large auditorium, various passengers sat watching the American film – which needed no concentration – and talking to each other in low whispers about the activities of the day. The smell of suntan oil punctured the air-conditioning, and the effect of bath essence and toilet water began gradually to luxuriate the air. The film was good, so were the seats. Most of those in the room were too old to be on the dance floor, and the darkened room and comfortable position were less disturbing than the nightly reminder above of their diminishing years.

Aliki, who had slept through some of the film and was now sitting near the exit ready to escape, wondered where in all this revelry was evidence of the sea. She slipped out of the room, climbed the inner stairway to the top deck and, leaning against a lifeboat, watched the ship's movement through the water.

Lifting her head, she gazed upwards and focused on a cathedral arch of stars. Suddenly the ship seemed very small and herself a dot on the seascape. Lowering her head she saw the compulsive pathway of the moon. She leaned further out over the rails to watch a deep fold of water curl round and burst in a low hiss.

Could she spend the night up here? She had so much more in common with the dark, the silver disc, the countless long-ago stars, than she had with the voices and rattlings down below. She put one foot up on the rail and behind her a voice called out, 'Watch out.'

Surprised, she fell backwards on to the deck and, pulling her dress around her, turned to see a slight figure stretching out a hand.

She rose awkwardly.

He picked her silk shawl off the deck and put it round her shoulders. 'Another moon-watcher,' he said. His teeth shone bright in the dark. She suspected he was laughing at her.

'I came up here to … to breathe. Down there,' she pointed, 'it's stifling.'

She could see he was studying her, but then he was walking away. Following rapidly, she walked step by step with him. 'Thank you for helping me. I wasn't really going to jump.'

He kept up the pace, neither inviting her presence nor yet rejecting her. Her steps hastening, she tried to examine his short figure, this man whose features were mostly hidden. Peering, she said, 'Have I seen you before?' She was not embarrassed by the triteness of her question.

He stopped, and as moonlight came from behind a cloud she asked, 'Are you Greek?'

'From Crete.'

'Like the captain.'

'The cradle of Western civilisation,' she said almost to herself, but was addressing his retreating figure. She called after him, 'What's your name?' but he had gone and she was left with the feeling of failed opportunity. Opportunity for what, she wasn't sure, but she felt it might not come again, and for some reason she wanted it to.

'Aliki.' It was her mother's voice. And again, coming nearer. ' What are you doing up here in the night air?'

'Looking at the moonlight spread across the sea.' She turned to face Audrey. 'It makes reality into a shadow.'

'And that's what you like, isn't it? Abstractions and unrealities.' Aliki felt her mother's hand on her arm, and looked up to see the slightly taller figure hovering there. 'We've made friends on this ship,' Audrey was saying, 'let's try to keep them.' Audrey flung her scarf over her head and, looking to see that Aliki was following, went down the companionway. On reaching the lower deck, Aliki noticed her mother greeting the interior warmth as if it were an old friend. 'They may soon give us up.' Audrey was still talking. Lecturing.

Aliki, who had thought herself to be part of an early dawn, found now that passengers in full evening dress were still jostling in and out of bars and gaming rooms. Some sat at tables and yet others were with a game of bridge. Generally speaking, it seemed that positions had been established for the voyage; groupings finished.

Audrey's voice, which had become a dull monotone, was saying, 'I came up to tell you that Peter Miller has invited us for a nightcap,' and Aliki, who was more inclined for a morning celebration, heard the familiar voice that came out through an open door. 'I'll order some drinks.' Seated at a table near the door, Peter Miller was bent over the backgammon board, and on the other side of it, Elena. The Major looked up and, lifting an arm towards an invisible steward, called out, 'Champagne for everyone?'

Elena's arm slid across the board, making a mockery of the move her opponent had just made. 'She's too bloody good,' he said, his arm as it were bringing Aliki and Audrey Martin in to the group.

Compelled now by the skill of the game, Aliki sat on the arm of Elena's chair.

'Thank you Major Miller, we'd like a glass of champagne.' Aliki noticed that the tone of Audrey's voice had altered. But why did she have to answer for them both?

She turned to watch the countess. Was she Greek? Was she Italian? Did it matter? She could see there was something timeless about her. Her skin had a richness, a soundness of texture that it was as if she carried sunlight in it. She was a sun goddess, night light very slightly diminishing the impact of her daytime well-being.

Elena's fingers moved backwards and forwards on the board, collecting, distributing. She was graceful in her movements and the Englishman sitting opposite, conscious of the honour she was bestowing upon him, had a glazed look of happiness in his eyes.

As the game neared its conclusion, Peter Miller's arm was less often in the air, and Aliki, sensing that perhaps the idea of a nightcap was more an emblem of friendship than an actual need for any more alcohol, stood up to say goodnight.

The Major rose and attempted a bow as Aliki crossed the room towards the welcome presence of the Friebels.

'Oh, how nice,' she beamed at them.

Professor Friebel moved to make room. 'We are having ... I think you call it a nightcap. Or, should I say, we have just had a nightcap and are on our way to salvage a little of the night in sleep.'

She moved closer, leaning towards them. 'Professor and Frau Friebel, may I come ashore with you both tomorrow?'

The professor stood up and, bowing slightly, said, 'Our pleasure. But what about the other lady ...?'

'She's heard the sea's rough round Delos. I don't think she will like it in the tenders.'

'Mrs Martin should come. Delos is the heart of the Aegean. A sacred island. In ancient times the centre of trading.' He smiled. 'Where trade was, there also were the temples. The merchants of long ago, as of now, were anxious to purchase security in both worlds.'

Aliki considered. Here was a balanced view of antiquity.

Standing beside her husband and putting a hand on Aliki's arm, Frau Friebel said, 'We must rely on the goodwill of the gods for our visit to the sacred island. It is never possible to rely on weather.' Her amused smile animated her face. Aliki turned to Costas, who was hovering close, and said, 'Costas, do you have a view as to who dictates the waves?'

The bar steward, smiling, said, 'The captain says it is unwise on a voyage to make mockery of the gods, even if, as we know, the gods themselves spend their day in a manner not unlike the passengers on this ship.' His grin widened.

'On Olympus', the professor joined in the fun, 'the gods make merry round golden tables where only nectar and ambrosia are served.'

'Perhaps for stronger meat they inhale whiffs of roasting flesh from the earth,' Frau Friebel ventured, her slightly quavering voice sounding carnivorous suddenly, and the professor, protesting, said, 'Not, surely, from human sacrifices.'

Costas, who had just opened a bottle of champagne in anticipation, poured now into each glass, 'Our captain,' he said, 'knows how to please such gods by accepting on their behalf the worship of most of the female passengers.' He let a few drops of champagne fall to the floor.

'And how do you see Olympus and the gods?' Frau Friebel leaned forward, and Costas, answering at once, said, 'Olympus is a glorified taverna where the gods, like the present-day Greeks, bargain and squabble and show pique, jealousy, lust and cunning.' He poured into another glass and, lifting it high, grinned and wished them all good health in Greek.

'The sailors on board this ship are more like a united family than a ship's crew.'

'The commanding officer of a regiment and the captain of a ship set the tone,' Professor Friebel said with satisfaction and, bending, helped his wife to her feet, settled his stick in his right hand and led the group out of the room. At the bottom of the stairway, Aliki stood watching the painful but determined ascent and the deliberate turning of the back to the ship's elevator, starboard.

Inside her cabin Aliki absorbed the silver light and felt the presence of the hovering moon. It was when she'd first read the Moon poem by Sappho that she'd had this feeling of oneness with Selene, who, because of her power, removed all colour beneath. She said the name softly into the room and then, speaking louder, intoned, 'Bright stars around the fair Selene peering, No more their beauty to the night discover, when she, at full, her silver light ensphering, floods the world over.'

Walking about the room – as if she could expand it – and with her eyes on the fresco on the wall, she felt life come once again into the cabin. Small Minoan figures walked through beautiful gardens. Elegant miniatures, golden-skinned, they smiled at each other and talked. She had no difficulty in blending these figures with the man she had seen – or partly seen – on deck. Smiling now at those who had come out of antiquity to greet her, she settled under the bedclothes and followed them through the gardens and into sleep.

Towards dawn, when Aliki and some of the other exhausted passengers were in the profoundest of sleeps, a storm developed. The restless among them felt vibrations and saw cabin curtains swing out from the ship's side and here and there an object slide across a dressing-table. Those who made the mistake of looking out through a porthole discovered their new angle to the sea.

'Take a good look at it.' Peter Miller was excited by the storm and annoyed by his wife's determination to use the occasion to vent her feelings on him. That he had come to bed late from his involved game of thrust and parry with the Italian woman did not seem to worry Daphne; that he had snored her awake did.

At home in East Sussex their rooms were even on different floors. Guests coming to stay would find themselves in an adjoining room to either wife or husband and with the intimacy of open-door conversation. Explanations of their sleeping habits were not given and, now that they were compelled to sleep in the same cabin, proximity was beginning to take its toll.

'If you'd drink less last thing at night, there would be less snoring.'

'What do you mean – drink less?'

'What I say.'

And they launched into the type of argument the pattern of which was familiar to both. In between these arguments they existed in a brother-to-sister relationship that was as companionable as it was unchallenging. In spite of the lack of sexual intimacy, Daphne Miller always managed to look the epitome of the well-loved and protected wife, Peter Miller the all-considerate husband.

'This is my holiday as well as yours, and if the enjoyment of it is increased by a couple of liqueurs after dinner then you can't really deny them to me.'

'But it's a couple of liqueurs after lunch, and then a drink or two or three early evening. Poor Molly is usually starving by the time we get to dinner.'

'Poor Molly Wainwright should be grateful that she's on this trip at all.'

'Peter!'

'Well it's true.' The hurt-boy look that followed this statement cancelled Daphne Miller's sisterly attitude in favour of her motherly one.

'Darling, you know how lonely and poor she is, and how much she appreciates …'

'… All right, but just remember that so long as you have your Molly, I shall have my drink.' Peter Miller slid down between the sheets and resumed his snoring.

Molly Wainwright was sitting up in bed looking out through the porthole when the knock came on the door. Stepping into her bedroom slippers, she said softly, 'Come in Daphne.'

She unlocked the door. Daphne Miller came carefully into the cabin, her legs moving as if they had iron in them, her arms outstretched for balance.

'God, what a storm!' She looked at the vertical black wall outside the porthole. 'Peter's snoring again and I can't sleep.'

Molly Wainwright moved to the side of the narrow bed and threw back the sheet. 'Get in. I expect it was really the storm that woke you.'

Daphne sat at the end of her friend's bed and examined Molly's face. She said, 'I've only come for a minute, the storm may get worse. Peter's on my nerves at such close quarters.' She turned to look at herself in the dressing-table mirror and, fluffing up her flattened hair, stretched an arm towards the other woman. They held hands.

'I'm so grateful for your understanding.'

'And I for your generosity,' Molly answered.

Lifting the glass of water that was beside her bed, Molly drank and said, 'I believe the captain quite fancies you. Did you see how he lingered over your hand at the end of the dance?'

'He lingers over every woman's hand.' They laughed and, taking a cigarette from her bag, Molly lit up.

'How *can* you at this hour?'

Ignoring the protest, Molly inhaled and said, 'Shall we go to Delos tomorrow?'

'We may not be able to.' Daphne looked at the black wall outside the porthole. But in any case, I'd rather take the opportunity to sunbathe on the deck free of all these people.'

'I thought you liked all the people.' Molly inhaled. 'Actually, Daphne, why are we on this cruise?'

'Peter answered an advertisement on impulse, and I said I'd go if you could come with us. It means we're together, darling.' Daphne ran a finger round the edge of her friend's face. 'And really we must be grateful to those who are absorbing Peter.'

'His overtures towards the Italian beauty are rather pathetic.'

'She's good for him.'

'She's good for everyone,' Daphne said in a wistful voice, gazing in the direction of the State Room.

Molly Wainwright stubbed out her cigarette. 'I don't think Aliki Findlay is impressed by the Major, but then he doesn't bother with her.'

'She isn't flamboyant enough.'

'Don't you think it's rather strange that that young woman is still travelling with her mother?'

'What age do you think she is?'

'Around thirty.'

'I doubt if they talk to each other.'

'Not like us.' They held hands once more and, looking towards the porthole and the angled curtains, put arms around each other laughing.

Daphne said, 'I think I'd better go.'

Molly climbed down from the bed, reached for her dressing-gown and put it round Daphne's shoulders. 'There,' she said, giving Daphne's neck a slight massage, 'you will feel warmer.'

'Neither Mrs Martin nor her daughter sunbathes.'

'Would you if you had their type of skin?' Both women looked into the dressing-table mirror and the reflection that came back to them told of sun hours together and contentment.

Daphne stood up. 'I'm glad I came. It's always such a restorative.'

'Leave Peter, Daphne.'

'You know I can't do that. He needs me.'

'Like a sister?'

'Yes.' She dropped the dressing-gown on the bed and moved towards the door.

'Poor Peter. Do you think he's actually enjoying himself?'

'Yes. Soon he will have manoeuvred himself into position as the most popular man on board.'

Stepping now with more confidence, a hand occasionally on the panelled wall, her eyes ahead of her, Daphne Miller went back down the passageway. Her thoughts played around the entertainment earlier in the evening, and her sexual dance with the captain. She knew that her bright colours were an immediate invitation to intimacy, the colours acting for her. She smiled a smile that changed to a small laugh: it was all part of the game.

On down the passageway, and bumping into the night steward for Upper Deck whose solicitous concern for her well-being inspired in her a slight feeling of guilt, Daphne hovered outside the stateroom that she knew to be shared by Elena and her rich American. They were an odd couple, but then …

Stepping quietly into her own cabin, she shut the door on the voices she heard coming from there.

In fact, inside the stateroom there was only one voice to be heard. It came from the unconscious mind of Carl Roberts. Late dinners followed by the inevitable bottle of champagne made sleep into a battleground of unrest. The following morning, pillows, sheets, on one occasion even the mattress, were on the floor, and Elena was bending over him laughing in her nakedness.

Now with a final shout that turned into a snort, Carl Roberts spoke. 'You say something, honey?'

Silhouetted against the black porthole, Elena's naked body roused feelings in the large recumbent figure that did not coincide with his wish to sleep. Recollection of their before-dinner coupling would have to suffice. Years of following after a pretty butterfly wife who wanted to make love only when the situation was bizarre had left him appreciating the comfort of a woman interested at any time. Elena was both sensuous and loving, giving the whole of herself to the person of the moment. Now, with his eyes shut, his body turned from her, he could restrict the vision to his mind. He thought of her detailed care for her body; of the massages, exercises, swimming sessions, painful removal of every hair and, with a sharp intake of breath, remembered the silken feel of the triangle between her legs. In about ten days' time this temporary loan would be giving ephemeral pleasure to someone else.

Elena turned from her study through the porthole and,

seeing the large bulk was not yet at rest, tiptoed to her own side of the double bed and slid under the covers. She put a protective arm round the man who was currently taking her on one of her favourite cruises. She felt a great affection for this large man who lay breathing – now evenly – beside her. Among the millionaires she knew, this one was the most generous. Breathing evenly now, with her arm round the large waist, she followed him into sleep.

On the bridge Captain Manoli, who had come up with the onset of the storm, spoke now to the officer of the watch. 'It may be worse before it gets better.' He looked at the chart. 'I'll be here for the remainder of the night.'

'Things are not going badly, sir,' the officer of the watch told the captain, and the captain, turning to the coxswain, said, 'What's our course now, Cox'n?'

'One eight seven, sir.'

'Port ten,' the officer of the watch answered him, and the coxswain said, 'Port ten, sir. Ten of port wheel on, sir.'

'Meet her. Steer one hundred and three.'

'Course one hundred and three, sir.'

'Hold her there,' the officer of the watch said finally, and the coxswain answered, 'Aye aye, sir.'

Taking another look at the heavy clouds around, but satisfied that the bridge had the situation under control, Captain Manoli stepped into his day cabin. He lit a cigarette, slowly blew out the match and thought of the scene he had been brought into an hour ago. It had begun when the Canadian girl, running up and down the Sun Deck shouting obscenities at the raging sea, had brought out members of the crew. Behind her on the deck, trying to steady herself, had been the older woman, clad only in a nightdress and dressing-gown, screaming for help, as the girl, with arms outstretched, had tried balancing on the ship's rail. A crew member had held on to her, at the same time shouting to an officer to bring the night nurse, and the night nurse in turn had sent for the doctor. A sedative had been injected into Tessa's buttock, but her leg reacting against it had shot up and temporarily concussed the member of the crew who had been holding her. The captain had been called in to witness the whole event and had been pleased to see that the incident had revealed a new sobriety in the doctor. All in all, the captain was quite pleased with the chain reaction brought about by the demented girl. It confirmed that discipline was strong on the ship.

But now, as the swell increased, the master of the ship was again in command on the bridge with the officer of the watch at his side. The navigator and communications seamen were also close by, together with an additional lookout and messenger. Deck officers were on duty and deep in the bowels of the great ship the engine-room watch was at its most alert as the massive hull dipped and bucked and shuddered its way through the storm.

The swell abating, the captain returned to his day cabin, lit another cigarette and, staring at the charts on his table, thought of the capriciousness of the gods. Libations had drenched the ground, virgins; he felt almost certain, had been sacrificed, and the Greek-born hostess who had given the lecture on Mykonos and Delos in the auditorium early in the evening had echoed the voice of Delos's subterranean cisterns to impress upon the rapt listeners that Delos was one of the sacred pulses of the world where even the act of love had to be deified. In the rational area of his mind the captain, of course, gave no credence to such musings, but in his heart he was always a little apprehensive of the storms in this area. In all the years of cruising with this ship, he had found that the island of Delos was so often a consort to the storm. Some could understand that it did not want visitors poring over its sacred parts. Stubbing out the cigarette, the captain shrugged his shoulders, laughed away his superstitions, but just for luck spat quickly onto the deck.

In the early morning, the storm clouds squeezed and knocked the ship and only with the first struggling upwards of shafts of sunlight did the sea finally settle and lay before the *Laconia* a grey but smooth path for its onward journey.

If silence can be said to be an actual phenomenon, then the

quality of it woke Aliki one hour before she was due to go ashore the following morning. A grey, almost pearly light was coming through the porthole and a film of damp coldness lay on top of the warm air. Surprising herself by the suppleness of her spring out of bed, she stood by the porthole trying to separate outline of land from horizon. The island of Delos was veiled from view but the pattern of hovering cloud told her that it was there. Touching her cabin wall aft, Aliki listened for the usually wide-awake pre-breakfast conversation. She looked at her watch: nine o'clock, it was late for them. The erratic snorts and snores from the Italians in the cabin forward gave reassurance that during the storm all had not changed. She slipped into a pair of cotton trousers and a T-shirt and wrapped herself in her towelling dress. It was cold for a swim but she wanted the spasm of excitement as warm flesh hit cold water. In a swimming pool or, better still, in the sea, one became conscious of the whole of oneself, head relating to toe, hand to leg.

She opened the door cautiously, expecting even at this hour to see Nikos hovering, and wondered if perhaps the Canadian girl had been exhilarated by the storm. How much of the hysteria, talk of ill-health, hatred – yes – of the woman with her were part of the symptom rather than the sickness itself? Since deciding to invite Tessa to her secluded corner on the Sun Deck, she had seen nothing of her. Her cabin door was open. Where was the couple?

Up and down the passageway, passengers moved with a new sense of purpose. There was a challenge in the air: would the islands be visible? Mykonos, one of the most beautiful of the Cyclades, with its many small white chapels and whirling windmills, lay smiling at its audience, and Aliki, now up on the Sun Deck, found herself smiling back. The small town was like an unfinished canvas set on its easel waiting for the artists to fill in colour and sketch out figures. Set against the ink darkness of the turbulent sea, the island was a gift of light, generated, it seemed, from its own centre. She continued to look. Soon, passengers would flood ashore, peopling the narrow streets, bargaining and talking in loud tones when language communication was poor. She felt the crushing weight of meaningless curiosity and, turning from the rail, walked into the middle of Carl Roberts's camera.

'Isn't that something!' He clicked with the camera, using Aliki as a foreground. 'You going ashore today?'

The large, solid niceness of the man dispersed her feelings of resentment and she came near to pleasure in the proximity of him. Dressed in a long white towelling gown, the girdle trailing the deck, the shock of unruly, sand-coloured hair standing straight up at the back of his head, he beamed. Aliki sensed the warmth of the shared bed he had just left — a faint odour of musk still lingering. Was she a little envious of the union that had taken place?

'Yes. I'm going ashore.'

'Then let's go get some breakfast.' He put his wide arm loosely round her waist and together they descended the companionway, not, as Aliki had meant, to the swimming pool, but into the dining-room, where greetings in French from a table near the door gave an unexpected and pleasant flavour to the morning. They chose a table beside the French family and idly Aliki picked up the day's menu for luncheon. Fried Frogs' Legs, Catsup Sauce, Veal Scaloppini Sauté à la Parthénope, Broiled Skewered Fillet of Beef, Souvlaki. Smiling, she passed the menu to Carl Roberts who, glancing at it, put it on the table face downwards.

Aliki looked up to see her mother come into the room followed by a man with a small moustache whose very neatness seemed to diminish his already small stature.

'Good morning, Aliki. Good morning, Mr Roberts.'

Aliki provided, and made room for them at the table.

Audrey held out her hand and, turning to the man standing hesitatingly beside her, said, 'And this is Mr Fosdick. We met last night at the bridge table.' Aliki was surprised to see her mother's social smile encourage them all to take notice of the small attentive man now putting her shopping bag on another chair.

'Can I persuade you all to indulge in a real English breakfast?' Carl Roberts patted his stomach. Aliki, seeing the calculating look in her mother's eye, noted that all her interest in Carl Roberts had disappeared. Carl, ignorant of what passed between the two women, ordered for himself bacon and eggs, with kippers to follow. 'Ah can see you all blanching,' he said, lifting the steaming jug of coffee brought by the steward and offering to pour.

The neat-looking man on Audrey's left cleared his throat, put his hand to his mouth and said, 'Excuse me, but I think we must be the only English on board.'

'Don't count me,' Carl Roberts grinned and, tying the girdle round his middle, loosened it again in anticipation of what was to follow.

'Oh no! There are others.' Audrey Martin's eyes searched. 'Quite a few in fact.' She spoke with her head turned just slightly from Mr Fosdick, occasionally glancing down her nose in his direction and trying by the very angle of her body not to see too much of him.

'I'm on my own,' Mr Fosdick said, 'since my wife died. Just a few months ago.' He coughed, his hand to his mouth. 'My friends all said I must travel to get out of myself. Meet people. Go about.' The friends, Aliki could see her mother thinking, had not offered to come with him; they'd probably helped to make arrangements for his cruise. Had probably said, 'Don't hurry back.' Aliki smiled at Mr Fosdick. 'How nice for you to be surrounded here.' If only her mother would take her expression of open distaste off her face.

'Henry is the name,' he said. 'My friends call me Harry.' The small moustache that balanced precariously on his top lip quivered with the excitement of introduction.

The steward returned with a plate of fried eggs and bacon and, under cover, two kippers. He placed it all in front of Mr Roberts like an offering. He knew Mr Roberts was Roberts of Texas Oil. From another tray he took more jugs of coffee and hot croissants, which he distributed round the table. Carl Roberts began to eat, and was silent and still chewing when the others at the table got up to leave. His hand stretched out to detain Aliki, and she, wondering if such obesity was a symptom of loneliness, or, more likely, just a strong liking for food, sat down again. In her experience of the rich she'd found there was a determination to show generosity before they could be suspected of the calculating meanness that had kept them rich. But now, as she watched Carl Roberts's appreciation of the food that had been presented to him, she felt certain that here was a rich man with a bent for kindness.

Aliki buttered another hot croissant, applied the Greek honey from a small pot shaped like a beehive and, watching her mother leave the dining-room followed by Mr Fosdick carrying her basket, said, 'I think my mother has found a companion.' She waited to hear if there would be any reaction from the man who was finishing his breakfast and was not disappointed when he said, 'Ah had difficulty in seeing him.' This time he laughed, picking some bones from out of his teeth. 'What I love about ocean travel is that you meet people who do not seem to exist anywhere else.'

'That is true,' Aliki agreed, got to her feet and offered a pat on the broad shoulder.

Catching up with Audrey on Verandah Deck, where many of the passengers had gathered to look at the condition of the sea between ship and land, Aliki said, 'I'll just change my clothes.'

By the time Aliki reached embarkation point on A Deck, the usual tightly knit crowd of sightseers had formed themselves into the continental answer to the English queue and were already pushing each other towards the exit. Individual voices rose from the general hum, of which the clearest was the sharp staccato from Peter Miller. 'I can't think why the purser doesn't issue tickets.'

'You mean go ashore by numbers?'

'Why not? At least it would be fair.'

'Vot is fair about numbers?' a guttural voice interrupted the dialogue. 'First to come, first to be served.'

'But that's the point, old boy.' Peter Miller's public school accent was strengthening. 'With you lot one might easily come first and still go last.'

Spotting Professor and Frau Friebel standing silently at the back of the crowd, Aliki joined them and sank back against the panelling. 'Let's hope word comes soon.' She smiled at the couple who stood patiently waiting.

'I am fearing the sea is still too rough.' The professor steadied himself against the wall.

As passengers grouped and regrouped and voices became petulant and impatient, word began to run through the ship that a further storm was developing some miles out to sea.

Up in his day cabin Captain Manoli was in discussion with his radio officer, the latter having reported from the wireless room that the forecast given out earlier in the morning had proved to be inaccurate.

'If we get them off at once they would stand a chance of reaching Delos before the storm breaks.'

'There's the journey back, sir.'

The undulation of the waves began to affect the ship and the captain, out on a bridge wing, felt the familiar thrill of excitement that accompanied confrontation with the elements. If Poseidon was going to tempt him this way, then soon – and why not now? – he would answer the challenge with a daring bid for supremacy at sea. He was about to cancel all disembarkation, both to Delos and Mykonos, and sail head-on into the storm, when the good sailor that he was silenced the angry Greek within, and he rapped out an order. 'Open the door for disembarkation to Mykonos. Cancel the tenders for Delos.'

With her back still propped against the pine panelling, Aliki listened to the professor on the subject of trading in ancient times, and when the news spread of the cancellation of the trip to Delos, Professor and Frau Friebel nodded to each other. She said, 'Now the tramplings and noise of the twentieth century will not upset the ancient spirits of the place.'

Limping slowly away, Frau Friebel beside him, the professor threw over his shoulder, 'In ancient times, and even without engines in their crafts, they were putting to sea in storms.'

'In ancient times,' Aliki answered him, a certain petulance in her voice, 'in ancient times they were not given weather reports.'

The professor and his wife climbed slowly up the companionway and Aliki, quickening her steps, went along the passageway to her cabin where Nikos, waiting for her, made the bed.

'Is sick in hospital.' He pointed out. 'Last night she go over the rails.'

'Literally?' Aliki's heavy-lidded eyes were wide open.

The steward, with arms outstretched, imitated the girl on the rails, and Aliki, mesmerised by the moving black stubs in his mouth, said, 'Okay, Nikos, I'm off to the hospital.' Hurriedly, she left the cabin.

Inside the hospital, which she found to be a pleasant large cabin with floral bedspreads and curtains, were two patients: Major Miller, sitting on one bed, and the other a body that seemed lifeless.

'Is it all right to come in?'

The doctor, who was bent over Peter Miller's naked back said, 'Please to sit down.'

Peter Miller's suntanned body had taken on a swollen and livid look in the lower left-hand corner of his back, and his face, registering pain, was at the same time covered in a look of righteous indignation. 'Bloody bee bothered to come off one of those islands to sting me.'

Aliki suppressed a laugh. She turned towards the silent, motionless body in the other bed. 'Hello, Tessa.'

Large vacant eyes stared. Aliki could hardly remember the animated hysteria of the encounter in her cabin.

'It's Aliki from the next-door cabin. Would you like ...?' What might the girl like? 'Would you like me to ... to read to you?'

Tessa nodded.

Aliki pulled the chair near to the bed and from her large canvas bag brought out her library book, *The Dawn of Civilisation in Europe*. She shut it. It was not the moment for such a book. Her eyes searched the room.

On the locker beside the other bed she saw an anthology of world verse. She glanced at the doctor. He nodded, then gave Major Miller a reassuring tap on the shoulder. 'It is good now.'

'Until some other foreign body fancies my sweet flesh.'

The Major, reassured now about the spreading poison, was prepared to joke, even to be flattered by the bee's attention. Putting on the brightly coloured sweatshirt, which he would never wear in England and which he donned as soon as he crossed the Channel, he went across the room in a couple of jogging strides and waved goodbye from the door.

Aliki leafed through the pages of the anthology, scanning lines. Halfway through, in Wordsworth's *Intimations of Immortality*, she found, 'And, even with something of A Mother's mind, And no unworthy aim, the homely Nurse doth all she can, To make her Foster-child, her Innate Man …' She looked up to see a flicker in the vacant eyes, and began to read.

But the doctor was returning, bringing a tray of drinks. He had become the host in the salon rather than the physician in his consulting room. Aliki wondered how he managed to function on the borderline of both. He'd brought in another chair and now pulled it close to the patient's head, and the smile that he gave encircled all three in a feeling of well-being.

The doctor poured from a whisky bottle.

Tessa sat up suddenly. 'If you were to take the needle out of my arm and remove the drip, it would make no difference.'

Aliki stopped reading and considered the situation; had the doctor expected this? Was such medical paraphernalia as he was using intended to preclude interference from predatory relations? Perhaps the doctor had guessed that the nurse was actually the girl's mother. Such fantasies were not unknown on board ship. She wondered if, in applying his psychological knowledge to the case, he had decided to appear essentially the physician.

'You are right,' the doctor answered finally, 'it would make no difference.'

'Thank you.' Tessa sat up. Doctor Anagnosti removed the drip. Tessa got off the bed where she had lain fully clothed except for one bare arm, and Aliki handed her her pocket book. 'Thank you.' Tessa stood tall and Aliki, putting her arm through the girl's arm, said, 'Let's go to Mykonos?' At the door she turned to look at the small ugly man with the radiant smile and silently thanked him for so much humanity.

Carefully avoiding any encounter with Audrey or a group she might be with, Aliki led Tessa out through the A Deck exit and into a waiting tender. Tessa held on to her arm as they made the journey to the island, and it was only when they were in the narrow streets that Tessa let go.

They walked slowly at first, fingering the goods that appeared to tumble out of the cavern-like shops on to the road. Tessa, gaining confidence, began to skip, then to run in and out of the small jewellery shops, sticking rings on her fingers and showing them, like a child who has just dipped into

Father Christmas's bag for all to see. What age is she, Aliki wondered; perhaps thirteen. She had not thought of her as pretty, but now the short hair, the result of Nikos's handiwork, and the sudden animation gave a sharpness that even the passers-by noticed.

A shout of pleasure from down the street told them that Carl Roberts was near. He was walking towards them and Elena, a few steps in front, was gesticulating and pointing to all she could see. The loose garment hanging from her shoulders and knotted halfway up one thigh revealed the lushly tanned legs, her slim feet thrust into open sandals of shining gold. Above them the clouds tussled and tore at the day, occasionally letting through a streak of light to balance on an olive tree.

'Hello.' They had caught up, and Tessa, lifting her right hand to be admired, said, 'Hi. Look at this.' The little silver ring sparkled.

Carl joined them on their walk and, at the corner of the two streets in a shaded patio, they saw Peter Miller drawing on his eighth cigarette of the morning. Aliki watched as he set his face in the direction of the sun. If the clouds should disappear he would be nicely placed for the morning's tanning. Daphne sat beside him, and two chairs away Molly Wainwright studied the ship's bulletin for news of activities in the evening. She read from it: 'Roman night. All passengers are welcome to this party, but entrance to the discotheque will be forbidden to those who are not dressed as Romans.' She held the sheet of paper out for all to see, including in her gesture the approaching four.

'Peter's brought fancy dress with him.' Daphne looked at the girl walking between Aliki Findlay and the Italian, and Aliki, taking hold of Tessa's hand, said, 'This is Tessa McAllister.' Just as the group was seated, the black cloud above exploded and, as rain washed the patio, all but Tessa made for the shelter of the restaurant. She stayed out in it, laughing and stretching her limbs to the rain, until Carl Roberts, unfolding a large raincoat, lifted her up off the chair and into the restaurant. Once inside, Tessa stopped laughing and accepted the black coffee that was being offered. She sat looking at Elena, whose cool hand was on her hot brow.

As suddenly as it had begun, the rain stopped and sunlight pierced branches of the orange grove and lit puddles on the ground. Round the corner of the patio, huddled together under a large coloured umbrella, Aliki spotted two figures coming into view: one tall, elegant, distancing herself, the other obsequious and attentive. 'Hello, Audrey.' Aliki moved to make a space for her mother and Mr Fosdick and watched with amusement as Fosdick put three packages on the table. Greek shop names were printed on the side of the bag and the bulging shape told the story.

Mr Fosdick hovered beside the table, running a finger round the edge of it.

'Sit down, man,' Peter Miller said eventually. 'What're you drinking?'

'A dry sherry would be nice.'

'You're not going to find sherry in this sort of place, old boy,' Peter Miller answered him, and, calling for the waiter, ordered two more double ouzos and two glasses of water. Mr Fosdick sat down abruptly.

The heat of the sun dried up the last damp areas around them and, with the contrast of temperature, the effect of the drinks and the feeling of well-being, a mood of repose, almost sleep, came on them. Aliki, shaking off the desire to sleep, looked towards the sea, and watched a dark-haired boy, naked to the waist, riding side-saddle on a donkey. He guided the donkey towards a solitary white windmill and went in through a gap in a whitewashed wall. The sails of the windmill spun round, slicing the air, and pieces of thatched roof fluttered in the breeze.

She moved forward suddenly. The island of Delos – as if in salute to the older, less historic island – glowed with an inner luminosity. She thought of its history, of the ancient myth that the island had drifted through the Aegean since the dawn of time; of Poseidon's gesture to anchor it to the seabed, and of how it had become the eventual resting place of Leto, the mistress of Zeus, who was born on the wings of the south wind and gave birth to Apollo there. She looked more closely: there were no buildings to be seen on the island, only the stark geological structure of rocks and, by contrast, a gently curving beach.

She smiled to herself, looked at the dozing figures around her, and wondered if their captain was in league with the ancient spirits of Delos. Were both he and the weather gods protecting it from invasion? Reaching to the ribbon currently tying back her hair, she undid it, shook her head and let the strands blow freely.

'Tomorrow,' Carl Roberts broke out of his partial sleep, 'we sail towards Mount Athos.' He lifted his camera to include the whole group and, grinning, as if to put the smile in for them, said, 'It's men only there.'

His grin widened and Elena, with an arm loosely round Tessa's shoulders, said, 'And on board there is to be a Lysistrata buffet for women only.'

'What, on this Spartan ship?'

'Perhaps you don't know that in the ancient Greek state of Laconia women enjoyed almost equal status to the men.' She laughed and those sitting around shared in it.

'I'll stay with the women,' Peter Miller said, and Aliki, who was enjoying the steam rising from her soaked body, ventured, 'You can't. Not unless you have agreed never to war again.'

'Careful,' Daphne Miller mocked, 'that could be an invitation to hear his war story ...'

'... Did I tell you about our landings in Crete in the war, and how we ...'

'... Okay, Peter, that's enough.'

Carl Roberts put his camera back into its case. 'Ah'm looking forward to an all-male atmosphere.' His eyes sought Elena's.

'Monks, you mean,' Peter Miller said, and Aliki, whose feelings of irritation towards the Major were bordering now on open dislike, said, 'Meaning that the two are not the same?'

'Exactly.'

'Many of our great guys have gone there to seek both inspiration and solace,' Carl Roberts said.

Silence followed.

'I suppose you know that the loo arrangements in some of those monasteries are so primitive that the drains lead straight on to the vegetable garden.' Peter Miller stubbed out his cigarette and pushed another into his holder.

'And what do you think is put on to the garden at home?' Daphne Miller's tolerant expression changed to one of pity. 'But of course you never come into the garden, do you?'

Tessa, who had been sitting silently, looking about her with a just-risen-from-sleep look in her eyes, said, 'Perhaps an area given over to meditation might,' she hesitated, 'be nice.'

The silence that followed this remark seemed embarrassing only to Peter Miller, who ended it with, 'I think it's time for lunch. Daphne? Molly?'

The three rose, Molly Wainwright moving a little reluctantly, but soon they were walking away, arms linked, and Mr Fosdick, who had apparently not felt it his place to join in the conversation, said, 'Such a gentleman.'

Elena stood up. 'If we sail at six I'm going to find a quiet beach now. Is anyone coming for a swim?'

'Oh yes. Me. Please.' Tessa stood beside the Italian.

'You go right ahead and have your swim.' Carl Roberts turned in his chair towards Audrey Martin and Aliki. 'Ah shall ask these two ladies to accompany me to lunch.'

'But ...' Audrey Martin began, and Carl Roberts added, 'And you too Mr ... Mr Fosdick.'

'No. Thank you.' He patted his concave stomach. 'I never take lunch. You see, my wife ...'

'Mr Fosdick,' Audrey Martin spoke with slow deliberation, 'it doesn't matter now what your wife would say.'

Mr Fosdick gave a cough, then another. He stood up, crooked his arm in the direction of Mrs Martin and said, 'Well, yes ... Yes. Yes. I would like to take a little luncheon.'

Aliki hesitated as Audrey and Mr Fosdick followed Carl Roberts out of the patio, then, slowly walking down the narrow street after them, she absentmindedly picked an orange out of a basket and began to peel it. A particular movement ahead caught her eye. She stopped, stared, then ran towards the corner of the two streets. Almost certainly she had seen the man who was on the deck several nights ago. She quickened her pace, looked to the right, to the left, saw Carl Roberts, her mother and Mr Fosdick disappear into a small restaurant where flower baskets almost obscured the doorway. But there was no sign of the small Minoan figure, not even among the crowds jostling in and out of the shops. She turned round to look the way she had first come and the road showed only evidence of departing figures into shops and cafés, not one of them looking remotely like what she regarded now as the man on the deck.

Reluctantly she walked in the direction of the restaurant where Carl Roberts was currently playing host, and, still chewing on the skin of the orange, wondered and *wondered* who was this person who was coming out of her dreams and into her consciousness?

Inside the small Greek restaurant, where bowls of black and green olives sat invitingly just inside the door, Aliki was warmly greeted by Carl Roberts, who had risen to his feet with the surprisingly agile movement she had spotted before and was indicating the empty seat at the table, as he now edged himself over to the larger one beside it.

'Carl,' Aliki said at once, realising that for the first time she was calling him by his first name, 'did you see a small man standing at the corner just there?' She pointed to the right of where they were sitting. 'I mean, did you see some-one who looked, well, different?'

Carl Roberts leaned towards Aliki, his grin sliding up his face, and looked towards the corner. 'Different from what?'

She thought for a moment and then said, 'I don't know exactly, but I see him every now and again, have spoken to him once on the ship, but it's as if he's not really on it.'

'You mean the guy's not a passenger?'

Mr Fosdick cleared his throat. 'Is he a foreign gentleman?'

'We're all foreigners here,' Aliki said and, seeing her mother wince, wondered if Audrey was developing a protec-tive attitude towards Mr Fosdick.

'It doesn't matter.' She spoke emphatically. She didn't want to share her phantom with all this cynicism. Carl Roberts closed the conversation by laughing and saying, 'In that case we won't have to sort out one Greek from all the thousands around.'

'The tenders that brought us here will be returning to the ship in about two hours,' Mr Fosdick reminded them, and with his fork and knife delicately poised he neatly removed the backbone from the fish that was now on his plate.

All, including Aliki, whose eyes no longer searched, put their minds to the task of removing the strong backbone from the red mullet Carl Roberts had ordered for them.

The storm that had kept the island of Delos free from alien feet had now moved west and was disappearing over Greece. As the *Laconia* set sail once more, plotting her way through some of the Cyclades, the captain stood on the bridge answering some of the questions from the large, red-headed American whom he'd invited up there. At first they'd sat in his day cabin, but Mr Roberts had asked to go out on deck where he could make good use of the evening sun by photographing the islands bathed now in a cyclamen light. One deck below they could see Peter Miller being humiliated once more by Elena over a game of backgammon and, sitting close to them with her eyes fixed on Elena, the girl, Tessa McAllister. Aliki was in a deck chair near the rails watching the sinking sun. She looked up and waved, and Carl Roberts beamed a greeting. From visits to other ships he had learned that the whole pattern of life was to be seen from the bridge. To the captain he said, 'You say the ship's twenty-three tons?'

'And one hundred and ninety-two metres long, twenty-four across, and was built in 1957.'

'That's okay, Captain, you can cut out most of the statistics. Ah'll ask what I want to know. Ah'm not just the touring American.' He leaned over the rail. 'How many can you get into the lifeboats?'

'The whole passenger list.'

Carl Roberts was making notes. He made notes all the time, notes of girls' telephone numbers, names taken from labels inside coats, books people recommended, sometimes even the date.

'How many seats in the life rafts?'

'All round the perimeter.'

'Is that right?' Carl Roberts smiled affably at the captain. The captain had asked him up here to show off his ship, and it was Carl Roberts's pleasure to be seduced. There were some who mistook the benign, indulgently overweight American for the innocent he was not. Carl Roberts, like most who have a great deal of money to protect, knew how to look after both it and himself very well. If he chose to hide behind a veneer of vulnerability then more fool he, or she, who fell for it. Captain Manoli understood pretty well the weight of the man who stood with him, and was pleased now to be discussing the ship, or anything for that matter.

Carl Roberts put the notebook away. 'Mah company is planning to buy a couple of cruisers. We hope to start up a line.'

Captain Manoli blinked almost imperceptibly. He saw a ship as a whole way of life, and it was difficult for him to imagine the purchase of two of them merely as an addition to the shopping basket.

'It's a great ship,' the American said, 'and you're running a good cruise.' His large hand with the fine red hairs on the back reached out. 'Thanks for all the information.' He went down the stairway, turned and, as if to lighten the mood, said, 'Will you be at the Roman party tonight?'

'Yes. Will you?'

'Aye, Claudius.' Carl Roberts knew the joke was thin, but it might just confound the captain, as his knowledge of both history and literature did others. Fat men, he knew, were supposed to be stupid. He'd always kept quiet about the three years spent at Cambridge, England, where he'd come away with a first-class science degree, and where he'd been involved with the literary club of the time. His accent could be as clipped and abrasive as the best of them, but the image of the slow-talking, drawling Southerner suited the idea he'd built of himself. What he liked about Elena was that she saw through it all and yet, paradoxically, he resented that there was no longer any actual mystery between them.

He came out on to the Sun Deck, decided against a ringside view of the slaughter of Peter Miller and went starboard along a dying sunbeam towards the woman on the ship who did hold for him something of a mystery. He stepped sideways, held his camera at an angle to the setting sun and, looking down into it, focused on Aliki. He saw there an expression that he'd never noticed out of the camera. He smiled to himself. If it weren't for the girl's mother, who was blatantly keen to push her daughter at him, he might just have stood a chance there.

'Do you come here often?' he tried on her, his words not yet dispelling the mood Aliki had created around her.

She turned and, standing up, levelled with him, saying, 'Not often enough.'

Together they stood by the rails and watched the thin silver shaving of the moon float up into the sky, in balance with the sun.

'It's not every day Ah get the chance to see a beautiful girl both under the moon and at the same time in the sunlight.' She smiled, and Carl Roberts touched her hand on the rail.

Behind them the deck had emptied, passengers having gone to their cabins or to the indoor swimming pool or for a massage. Carl Roberts did not invite her for a drink or make any suggestions at all and, as they walked together across the deck, his arms hung loosely, penguin-like, at his sides. If he had touched her again it would have been all right, Aliki decided.

She said, 'See you later,' and moved towards the interior stairway. Carl Roberts, watching her descend, said, 'Yeah.'

Inside her cabin, where the only light was through the porthole, Aliki lay on her bunk, wondering. On deck she had been watching the movement of the sea not only because of itself but also because it was helping keep motivation going for herself. A backward look into her life had shown her something of her dumb acquiescence. Now, she felt, was her chance to promote self-generated activity.

According to Audrey, her own childhood had been marred by the recurring illness of her father, Aliki's grandfather. Aliki had come to know him through the books, some of which were now in Audrey's library, crammed into the London flat. With the collapse of her grandfather's health had come the deterioration of the estate, and when the house and property were sold various members of the family had taken most of the books. Recently she had discovered a leather-bound diary in which she had found the truth about her grandfather. From various scribbled entries she had learnt about the approaching insanity, about his visits in and out of homes. Further research had revealed mainly incoherent letters from the hospital, and these had led to further investigation into the whole desk. There were bills. The last bill, dated the first of the month on which they were travelling, had told her that her grandfather was still alive.

She sat up suddenly. Why had Audrey hidden the truth? Why had she not told her that this gentle, artistic man had become a deranged shell? Why? It had taken a couple of days of consecutive thinking to work out a little of Audrey's predicament. Her mother's attitude to her father's condition was not so much one of shame as of fear. Fearing for her own stability, she had shut her mind to the truth. A feeling near to sympathy had taken hold of Aliki and she had decided to postpone confrontation until after the voyage. Now, several weeks on, she had the strength to confront Audrey. Was this ship some sort of catalyst for change?

She could hear Tessa's voice coming through the wall. It was calmer now and the answering voice was one of complicity. The sound was of a duet, an air from an old theme, resung.

The ringing of the gong for the first sitting for dinner carried down the passageway, and Aliki could hear doors opening.

A faint rhythm, perhaps the basic throb from the engines, was coming into her room. Perhaps it was the bazouki accompanying the Greek dancing in the Verandah Bar. She turned on the small light by her bed and looked at the bulletin for the evening: the entertainments officer would be teaching his Greek dancing class, and the passengers, arms out and around each other's shoulders, would be moving forward, some in time, others struggling to keep up. She kept time with her foot. Had the idea of dance come from the land of the goddess Rhea, who had taught the Curetes in Crete to clash their arms on their shields to conceal the birth cries of the infant Zeus and so save him from his devouring father, Cronos?

The beat was stronger now.

In time, the Cretans, with their sense of a single divinity in all things, realised that the all-pervading creative power was for them ... feminine. Aliki stood up. The mother-goddess was of a domestic divinity, as well as a divinity of the wild places, and of the unconscious mind.

'Things went wrong when the male gods arrived, bringing their glorification of war,' she said into the room.

She stood still in the space between bunk and porthole. Were not both earth and water recognised in the human psyche as feminine elements – in contrast with air and fire, which were masculine? The closer one came to the former, the greater the feeling of oneness.

No wonder she liked swimming. She tiptoed about the room. How great were a people who did not glorify war? Had not the Cretans reduced and diverted their aggressiveness through a balance of the physical and the spiritual, striving, perhaps, for perfect balance.

Yes. Their enthusiasm for sport, games and above all dancing, all connected with it. She moved freely about the cabin now, her arms swinging. Perhaps her study of the Minoan period in history was a sign that she was coming up out of her own dark age.

She sat now in front of the looking-glass, brushed her hair, absentmindedly put cream on her face and stared at her reflection. Was she interested in the Minoan civilisation because of their acceptance that death was part of their culture? Or was she a little in love with a people who saw beauty through into death? Either was seductive.

The telephone rang and she stared at the instrument, willing it to stop. The unspoken words, appearing like symbols of music on a sheet, danced in front of her. She already knew the conversation that was to follow. No, I don't want to go to any party tonight. But, darling ...

'Hello? Yes?'

'Mr Roberts has asked us all to go to his stateroom for drinks.'

'Us all!' So they had become a group. Well, she was happy for her mother and hoped it would support her through the following days because she was not going to join it. She was going to ...

'I think I'll give it a miss.'

'But it's you he wants to see.'

'It's no good, Audrey, I'm not interested.'

'You never are.' The voice was sharp, and Aliki felt upset because she liked Carl Roberts and would be happy to have his attention, if only...

'Think of all the other interesting people you might meet at the party,' Audrey pressed.

'All right, Audrey, I'll think of them and you can go and meet them.' Sometimes she was childish in her responses to her mother, snapping out the pert retort. Now she decided to confound her. 'Actually, I'm meeting someone on deck.'

'Meeting someone on deck!' Audrey's voice was incredulous. 'Who is it?'

'Just someone I met the other evening.'

'Male or female? Is he English? Greek? Or what? I do think you might have told me...'

'... If you really want to know, I've got a date with Selene, the moon goddess.'

'Oh no, Aliki, not that again.' The flatness in her mother's tone nearly touched her. Twisting the telephone to her other ear, she reached for the fresh lime drink on her bedside table. The half-moon, brighter now, was centred in the porthole.

'See you tomorrow at breakfast,' Aliki spoke directly into the mouthpiece. 'Good night, Audrey.'

She lay down again and turned off the light. This was not the aloneness of isolation. It was the aloneness of expectation; she would make something happen. Tomorrow when the men on the ship poured into the sacred peninsula of Mount Athos she would have a proper date with the sun, lie fully under its rays, tan a little …

She got off the bed and turned on the light, changed her drink from lime to whisky and pressed the bell by her bed marked 'dining-room steward'. She would have dinner here. Tomorrow, up on the Sun Deck, she would study Elena and watch how she managed both to draw from and give back to the life around her.

With the change in temperature and the disappearance of all signs of humidity, Professor Friebel was moving more freely about the ship. Frau Friebel – a constant watcher for signs of fatigue – had agreed that, yes, an early morning swim in the indoor pool, when the rest of the ship was asleep, might, indeed, be a good idea. Apart from some pleasant but brief exchanges with the young Englishwoman, whose interest in Greek antiquity excited the professor, the couple had kept their own company. Frau Friebel had been amused by her husband's wish to attend the auditorium lectures on the places they would visit; in Bavaria it was he who gave the talks, incorporating into them his current view of political philosophy in connection with the Greek classical period. It had been her idea that they save up for a journey in comfort rather than make a hot trip across Europe in their small car, with the probability that her dear husband at the end of it would be too physically disturbed to study ... Now, as a result of an error of judgement on her part, the professor was stretched out on two chairs on the Sun Deck, his eyes torn with longing, Aliki Findlay close beside him, her eyes also glued to the secret peninsula.

The previous day, when the storm at sea had prevented the visit to Delos, Dr and Frau Friebel, deciding against a tour of the more popular Mykonos, had settled themselves on the Verandah Deck starboard, away from the sight of disembarking passengers but in full view of the capricious island, should it appear. One or two stewards had offered drinks, hot or cold, and the odd wandering passenger attempted conversation. But the large grey head bent in full concentration over some files, on which a neat, intelligent handwriting could be seen, proved a strong discouragement. Around eleven o'clock, when conditions on deck had become a little cold for relaxation, the doctor had risen surprisingly nimbly to his feet and announced his intention to go for an indoor swim. Alert at once, Frau Friebel had risen to offer help and was restrained by his free hand.

'Thank you, but today I manage by myself.'

Frau Friebel had watched nervously as he limped away. When a few minutes later the call for help came, she had rushed after him. In trying to avoid the clutter of passengers on the stairway the professor had turned inwards, his grip on his stick slackening for a moment, and had tripped over an unseen step. He had fallen head first, fortunately only on to a small landing, and had lain helpless but conscious. When one of the ship's officers had come to his aid, the professor had tried to make light of the accident. Two of the ship's officers and Frau Friebel had carried him into the lift, his wife actually just holding his hand, and into the surgery, where, once it was established there was no serious damage, the professor had had a restorative conversation with Dr Anagnosti, who seemed pleased to have a professor to question.

The fall seemed to release further intellectual energy in the professor, and in English – fluent on his part and halting on the Greek's – they discussed Homer's great epic, both *The Odyssey* and *The Iliad*. The ship's doctor, whose job it was to be adaptable to all subjects at any time, and who sensed that here was a scholar who needed balm for his pride rather than treatment for his bruise, tried him out on something that had cropped up with the English lady when she'd lingered a few days ago in his surgery. He poured whisky into two glasses.

'Dr Friebel,' he looked up at the tall man now sitting in a chair, 'how is it that the plot of the Iliad turns on the beauty of Helen and the plot of the Odyssey on the romance between Odysseus and Penelope, when we know that the idea of romance was, and is, *absent*,' the doctor seemed pleased he had got that word out, 'from all true Greek art and literature?'

Dr Friebel drank from his glass, looked at the astute-looking Greek and said, 'I think you know that both *The Iliad* and *The Odyssey* were about loyalty and love, not romance.' He moved his leg to a more comfortable position in the chair. 'But,' he said, looking seriously at the doctor, 'it is difficult to experience accurately the time about which Homer writes. The great epic was written a few hundred years after the siege of Troy. And we know, do we not,' he twinkled at the doctor, 'that the siege of Troy was not about Helen but about trade routes.'

Doctor Anagnosti smiled to himself, topped up his glass and said, 'I think some of the virtues of classical Greece are with us still.'

'These are?'

'Moderation, self-knowledge, self-restraint,' Doctor Anagnosti said, and when he saw the professor's eyebrows go up, he qualified by saying, 'Practical, unsentimental commonsense is still a main characteristic of our people.'

The two drank comfortably together.

Conversation had drifted into speculation about the likelihood of there being more than one Homer, and when the doctor suggested that Sappho was in a *group* of lyric poets, the professor agreed, 'There is seldom a time of isolated genius.'

Reunited with his wife in the comfort of their own cabin, Dr Friebel told of his interesting meeting with the ship's doctor, and Frau Friebel, listening to her husband's exposition of it, said, 'Yes, dear, but what did he say about your fall?'

Reluctantly the professor had to admit that he had been cautioned not to leave the ship for a couple of days.

Now on deck, his eyes longingly on what he remembered to be the strangely feminine-looking coastline of Mount Athos, Dr Friebel thanked God for the reassuring, unromantic, essentially practical love of his wife. He turned to the young woman sitting near to his chair and continued the conversation he had begun with her a couple of days before.

'Did you consider Mykonos to be any replacement for the failed visit to Delos?'

'It was lovely: whirling small windmills, whitewashed houses, thatched roofs and a background of sapphire sea, but,' and she looked at him, 'there was no mystery.'

The professor leaned forward to get an even better view of the approaching monasteries and Aliki, reaching into her string bag bought in Mykonos, brought out the suntan oil that Elena had given her. She poured and stroked and rubbed the oil into her skin, at the same time watching movement between the ship and the peninsula. Then, standing, she saw a thick growth of cypresses round the first monastery and, appearing above it, a solitary tower that displayed tiny windows and helped to give the impression that chants and prayers and thoughts and meditation were constantly circulating within. Other monasteries came into view, different only in size, but all with the same air of secret benevolence.

They dropped anchor about a quarter of a mile out from land, and as soon as the male passengers departed in lifeboats, the scene on the Sun Deck took on the sensuous, languorous atmosphere that Aliki felt would be found in the inner sanctum of a harem. She lay with other passengers, some luxuriating on their backs in the water, others on towels face down. A sprinkling sat under umbrellas or even further into the shade, and elderly matrons in less revealing swimsuits indulged in romantic novels normally hidden from husbands. Aliki noticed that conversation was general but light-hearted, and sentences of an intimate nature hung provocatively in the air.

Getting up to join the Friebels, she listened as Elena talked in a soft voice to some of the younger women, the silver eye-shadow that she wore at night replaced by a blue to match the sea, the scant two-piece of the same colour. Her blonde hair was knotted on top of her head, to minimise the area of shade Aliki, supposed, and the sun oil on her bronze skin sparkled in the sun. The small breeze that seemed to be around her was accepted as a caress, and, seeing her like this, Aliki wondered with amusement what effect she was having on the male potency of the peninsula.

'Have you met Maria Christina d'Capatorre?' Aliki stretched out her arm, and Elena, spotting the professor's intention to get to his feet, crouched beside him, smiling and gesticulating. Professor Friebel, allowing the feline effect of her to reach him, turned to his wife and said, 'To think that I am viewing Mount Athos in the presence of so many beautiful women.' And then he said to Frau Friebel questioningly, 'Athena?'

Frau Friebel, who had noticed Elena from the beginning

of the voyage and had sensed her radiance, said, 'Yes.'

Touching his shoulder briefly, Elena rose from her crouched position, saying, 'I shall block your view of Mount Athos,' and disappeared into the pool.

Deck stewards appeared with white cloths and began to dress the long, narrow tables placed under the covered section of the deck.

'May I get you something?' Aliki once more offered to serve the German couple, and Frau Friebel, turning from the scrutiny of the monastery, said, 'We eat lunch very little, but please may we offer you a nice cool drink?'

'Drink! Yes, a drink!' Major Miller's voice splintered into the gentle conversation and, as heads jerked round, the Major was observed dragging a chair from the deck starboard. 'Yes, it's high time we had a drink,' he called out and placed his chair in among the women. He held up his hand for a steward. 'Daphne! Molly!' The two women pulled chairs across the deck and sat on each side of him. They smiled apologetically at the gathering of sunbathers, and Aliki shrank into her chair as she heard Molly Wainwright say to the professor and his wife, 'Peter says nothing would get him into some damned monastery smelling of urine.'

'Oh dear.'

Aliki saw a small shudder go through the professor's system and she watched as, leaning back, he closed his eyes.

The honeyed atmosphere seemed to be shattered into fragments until Tessa, stepping out on to the deck wearing a long kaftan which tripped her as she walked, attracted their attention. Aliki saw that the jagged hair was flatter now, the expression on her face expectant but calm. She walked to the space between Elena and the pool and, pulling off the kaftan exposed a thin, white body. Eyes turned to the golden body beside her and all watched as Elena, pouring from a bottle, began to caress the exposed areas of Tessa's skin. The circular movement had a soporific effect on those watching and dispelled for the moment the abrasive effect of the Millers. The Major's arm dropped, the chattering ceased and all sank into a mood of sensuous well-being.

Surprised by the indolence of the passengers in the face of the enticements on the tables, the stewards filled plates with rice and raisin salad, stuffed vine leaves and vegetable pancakes, and offered them here and there on the deck. The passengers accepted the food at last, washed it down with glasses of iced wine and were ready, when a shout indicated the vociferous return of their men from the peninsula.

Emerging now from a partial sleep, Aliki was surprised to hear the pleasant tones of Carl Roberts declaring to the group:

'Well, Ah will be going back there one day.' The American was first up on deck and, dropping into a chair near Aliki, grinned encouragingly at those wishing to question him.

'You're out of your mind, old boy. The bloody monks would never encourage a second visit.' Peter Miller faced Carl Roberts.

The American patted his stomach affectionately. 'Ah'm just the sort of hedonist they'd love to get in there.'

'What I'm saying is,' Peter Miller was now standing above Carl Roberts talking down to him, 'anything unnatural can't be right. It can't be natural to herd a lot of men together in conditions not fit for animals.'

'The monks look contented,' came a male voice from the other side of the deck.

'Perhaps. But you can't expect moral benefit from a group of mentally sick men.'

'The conditions are no worse than in some of your public schools,' Carl Roberts intervened. The professor and Frau Friebel exchanged a smile, the professor at last having opened his eyes. The American continued, 'The emphasis in these monasteries is to free the mind from its bodily care in the cause of humanity generally.'

'What can a lot of unwashed, starved, self-denying would-be perverts know about humanity? Bloody unnatural. Not a woman in the place. Even the animals are male.' Peter Miller was now pointing his cigarette at the American, and his voice was rising. 'How the hell do they keep continuity? I suppose market day on the mainland is a sort of free-fucking for all.'

'... Darling,' Daphne Miller had risen and had her arm on her husband's. 'There is no need to get so excited. It's not as if anyone is asking you to go there.'

Aliki wondered what was so essentially frightening to Peter Miller about an all-male gathering. She watched as he picked up Daphne's handbag and, unzipping it, took from it the bottle the doctor had prescribed for his bite. Silently Daphne began to rub the painful area.

All round the deck male passengers were returning from the monastery, talking with excitement to their women, the women now resuming attitudes of interest, their faces set for listening.

Carl Roberts rose from his chair and, stepping lightly across the deck, reintroduced himself to the German professor and his wife and, in answer to the professor's request, 'Please, every detail', began his account of the visit to the monasteries.

The professor enjoyed the quiet American drawl and, turning to look at his wife, saw that she was listening intently.

Gradually the familiar throb and vibration from below gave indication that the ship was ready to sail, and, looking towards the starboard lounge, Aliki watched Audrey appear out of the door, joined by Mr Fosdick. She looked with amazement at her mother's bright yellow sun-dress, and observed the waiting figure of Mr Fosdick in magenta trousers and an orange T-shirt.

'Hello, Aliki,' Audrey Martin said, 'I've decided to start a tan.'

Aliki studied the unnatural high colour in her mother's cheeks, the more than usually elaborate hair and wondered if it were possible that her mother's wish to be part of a group was altering in favour of a desire to be one half of a two-some. Somehow she could not believe in this new interest in Mr Fosdick, though his warmth of attitude towards her mother seemed genuine enough, the ridiculous ornamental appearance of the man all part of the compliment to her.

She watched as they slid two deck chairs to a quieter part of the deck, and, dropping into them, turned to each other in conversation. She wondered what they found to talk about with such animation.

She now moved her chair fully into the sun, removed her sun-hat, put on the large sun-spectacles she had bought in Mykonos and thought to herself, Had she invited her own feeling of isolation?

The ship shuddered, turned starboard, became fully under sail and set a course for Istanbul.

The sail through the Dardanelles was at night, and Peter Miller, who had planned to give his group of friends a discourse on the unsuccessful but courageous British landing at Gallipoli in 1915, was, happily for Daphne Miller, deep in sleep. Earlier in the evening he had lost his temper when some Frenchman had accused Winston Churchill of mishandling the whole affair. 'It was that damned Liberal Lloyd George who was the real Judas in the affair,' Peter Miller had answered, and it had taken persuasion and guile from both of his women to prevent a tirade on the subject of wishy-washy liberalism, which inevitably would have led to another on socialism and finally communism.

The large white ship, lit by its own interior, sailed on

through the dark night, delicately positioned in the narrow straits, and most of the passengers were asleep. Aliki, who had asked for an alarm call around five-thirty, was at five o'clock fully awake. She was not going to miss the entry into Istanbul. She pulled on a sweater, slipped into a pair of jeans and moved silently out of her cabin. For once Nikos was not there and the night steward showed no surprise to see her. She climbed the inner stairway, and could see from the opaque quality of the light coming through an exit that she was just managing to beat the dawn. Stepping out on to the deck, she looked about to see if she was the first passenger awake and if, perhaps, her mysterious contact was somewhere to be seen. She walked to the rails and as her eyes became accustomed to her surroundings, blankness became shape. Looking over the rails, she could see gradually the ship's movement through the curling, silk-like surface of the Sea of Marmara. 'Marmara,' she said softly into the breeze, and lifted her head to greet the morning. Warm air hovered above the ship, reluctant perhaps to meet the cool of the water, and a huge travelling dart of light penetrated the dark ahead. Outlines of pink, purple and brown appeared on the port side, and further off a thin rim of gold balanced on the horizon. All around, minarets and domes began to emerge out of the scented sleep of the night and Aliki, who was coming awake with it, felt herself to be part of this scene of architectural wonder, East and West together. As light became a great blaze across the sky, the city of Istanbul was there revealed, secure in its sixteen hundred years of history. She stood hardly daring to breathe.

'What do you think of it?'

He was just to the right of her, standing relaxed by the rails, his head turned in her direction. She had not seen him since Mykonos.

'Yes, it's as if Istanbul has put on a display just for us.'

'It radiates for those who appreciate it.'

She said, 'Where do you get to during the days?'

'Sometimes I am on deck, but only in the morning and in the evening.' The English accent, she thought, was too correct. Now that the pink morning had turned to gold, she could look at the man and observe the strong body, dark, curly hair, light russet skin and neat features. But he was beginning to walk away, and she moved quickly after him.

'Please. Where can I find you?' she called out, and, turning, he answered, 'Don't worry.' He went down the stairway.

She stumped down the stairway after him. Who did he think he was, this ... this man from Crete? This modern-sounding, ancient-looking person? What did he do that he appeared only at night or in the early morning? Was he a writer? Perhaps a composer? Coming up on deck when he knew there'd be no one about.

He had gone, and she came back on deck. She stopped now by the rail and held on to it.

The great dome of the Blue Mosque came into sight, an outline rich even in this skyline, and behind it the strangely similar Byzantine one of St Sophia.

'Hi, Aliki.' Carl Roberts had come round the deck, wearing a buttercup-yellow suit and a wide grin to match the effusion of it.

She felt a sudden warmth for this man, whose reality was of the essence of morning. He said, 'Ah've been on deck for some time taking snaps.'

'But the light has only just...'

'Ah have a good camera.'

'Did you see me talking to a small man? Here. Just now. He's only just gone.'

'Ah was on the other side of the deck, honey. But Ah thought Ah heard voices.' He was focusing his camera on to the eastern side of the Bosphorus, pointing into the thick skyline of minaret and mosque, and working quickly to catch the changing light.

'Ah left Elena running off the hot-water system.'

'Oh?'

'If there's one thing Ah can't understand about that woman it's her inability to go to bed at night.'

'Goddesses don't need sleep,' Aliki said, and voiced the idea that Doctor Friebel had put into her head. 'She's the most,' she thought for a moment, 'sunlight person I have ever seen.' She was walking in step with him round the deck, and then stopped. 'I can't imagine that with Elena there are any grey days.'

'You're right.' He stopped and she with him. He said suddenly, 'Do you live with your mother?'

'Oh, no.' The idea of it shook Aliki, as did her denial of the truth.

'Ah thought you two were, well, sort of like contemporaries.'

'That's the trouble.'

He snapped the camera case shut. 'Ah'll be coming to London soon to see mah man of business. Ah'd like to see you there.'

'I'm living in my mother's flat just for the moment,' she confessed. 'She's been very kind to me since my husband died.'

'If that isn't the darnedest thing. You married!' He lifted her left hand. 'No band on the wedding finger.'

'I was married for ten years,' she said, and tried to think of some outstanding feature of it. 'Arthur was away a lot, so...'

'...You got into the habit of going abroad with mother.' He grinned and, seeing the stewards arrive on deck with trays for the Early Bird breakfast, stopped talking and looked to see what was on the trays. She studied the man beside her and wondered why she didn't resent his mockery.

As they moved towards the table, covered now with pots of coffee and tea, rolls and Greek honey, she decided to take the subject away from herself. 'Have you always been interested in food?'

'Ah'm just the fat boy who never grew up. Besahdes,' he drawled, 'when you ah as rich as Ah am you can do what you like. Mind you,' he continued, pouring from a coffee-pot into two cups, 'obesity is becoming the American sickness and Ah can't say Ah approve of that.'

'Where do you draw the line?'

'In here.' He pointed to his head. 'Ah could stop if Ah wished.' He grinned his crooked grin. 'Ah'm not eating to compensate for anything. I just like food.'

Aliki felt flattered by the honesty. And amused.

They drank coffee, munched rolls and poured on honey.

'Well, Ah'll be going now for a shower before having mah breakfast.' His laughter lingered with Aliki and stayed with her as she regarded the ship come alongside the quay. Others had come on deck to watch, and conversation ceased as the impact of the historic city reached them. Shimmering now under a heat haze, it gave out an aura of musk, petrol fumes and old mutton fat. Beneath the skyline of cupolas and mina-rets and white-colonnaded palaces, a congestion of black rotting wooden buildings would be hidden from view.

Large coaches waited on the quay to conduct passengers around the city, and Aliki, reacting against the sight of them, turned to see the captain standing, relaxed, on one of the wings of the bridge. She smiled up at him. He saluted and smiled a greeting.

This morning Captain Manoli was in a sanguine mood. Last night there had been a temporary scare when the night watch had reported a wild party on the top deck, starboard. The captain, on his own, had put a stop to the celebrations by inviting the whole group up to both his day and night cabins. The bunch of animated and highly tanned young men who had come on board at Venice, with a group of girls look-ing like a chorus line from an American musical, and who had all stuck exclusively to each other, had waited until most of the ship was asleep to start their acrobatics. Surprisingly they had not spilt drink or made a mess of his ship; drink, so the captain had observed, seemed to be an unnecessary addition to the vitality of such a party. He had greeted them all with extreme politeness, saying, 'Why restrict yourselves to the Upper Deck when you can view the scene from the bridge?' In strict order they had climbed the stairway and had enjoyed this 'crow's nest' of a view of the moonlit, star-bright sky, and eventually had all returned to their cabins mostly happy and mostly sober.

And now the captain was further pleased as the ship had made a good docking, the bridge and the engine-rooms working well together, and the large white ship, probably the most elegant in these seas, had made a sensational and well-observed entrance into the harbour. Wearing the tropical rig of the day – neatly pressed white trousers and shirt – he stepped down from the bridge on to the Sun Deck, where his crisp and consoling appearance was a reminder to those still questioning their future movements that here was security, and that there was no need to go into any evil-smelling and foreign-sounding bazaar if they didn't want to.

Now he exchanged excessively warm greetings with a group of German passengers, compensating in this manner for the slights they said they had been receiving at the hands of the ship's company.

'Bitte, Frau Hoffman,' he intoned to the pretty, plump, excitable woman in the purple sundress. 'Frühstück wird auf Bestellung in Ihrer Kabine serviert.'

'Nein. Nein. Today I ring three times and still it does not come.'

'Forgive us, Frau Hoffman,' the captain followed the German lady into English, 'but today our early morning sail into Istanbul occupied the stewards with early breakfast on deck.' The captain smiled sweetly towards the purple dress and, bowing just enough to satisfy the bruised ego, walked slowly towards the next bunch of hovering and, this time, smiling passengers.

'I do not know if that was a rebuke,' Frau Hoffman said in German, 'but tomorrow I know my breakfast will come on request.' She smiled a fat dimpled smile in the direction of the erect white back, and told Willy, her husband, that the captain was the only person worth dealing with.

'Dear,' Willy Hoffman said unsympathetically, 'you can lie in bed in the morning at home. Here we have come for the sights.' Frau Hoffman reminded Willy that two marriages back she had done this trip on her honeymoon

Aliki, who had overheard the captain's conversation with the Germans, wondered, as she saw him approach, if Captain Manoli was old enough to have experienced the German invasion of Greece in the last European war. There was just a slight air of resentment on the ship towards the German passengers, which was veiled because as a race they came in their numbers, took a great deal of interest in the sights belonging to the ancient past and, above all, she imagined, spent money.

The captain stood, as it were, to attention. 'Would you care to dine at my table tonight?'

She turned towards him. 'That's kind of you, Captain

Manoli, but this evening I am going to give dinner a miss.'

The captain, who was not used to having his invitations turned down, stood silently looking at his passenger. And the passenger, who had made her decision over her second cup of strong coffee last night, remembered her slight feeling of nausea. Last night's dinner, along with the five previous, had been more of an inducement on the menu than an actual gastronomic feast.

Cuisses de Grenouilles Frites had turned out to be fried bits of some unknown fish accompanied by a glutinous sauce probably straight from a bottle. Brochettes de Filet de Boeuf Grillé had been a sinewy stew, the Profiteroles au Chocolat, Crême à la Vanille, which Audrey chose whenever they went out at home, had been made, she decided, from a leftover of Yorkshire pudding. She knew that there was too much food offered all the time, and the novelty had worn off.

'Mrs Findlay, it is always possible to order exactly what you want to eat. Veuillez vous adresser au maître d'hôtel pour vos menus de régime.'

She was both touched and flattered by the captain's use of French. 'Oh, I'm not on a diet,' she protested. 'It's just that, well, perhaps I was a little greedy last night.'

'You understand,' the captain was now at his most benign, 'that meal-time is a great feature of any cruise.'

'I find the wines lovely,' she reached for an apology and the captain, his face breaking into a smile said, 'Ah, yes.'

'Very cleansing,' she added, remembering the expression she had heard from Peter Miller.

The smile on the captain's face vanished. 'The Greek wines are supposed to be a nectar, an ambrosia ...'

'You don't believe all that sort of thing, do you?'

'Mrs Findlay, it is my business to believe everything about Greek taste past and present.' His arm circled. 'And when you look around you here,' he looked towards Istanbul, 'and inhale the odours,' he sniffed, 'that are part of,' he hesitated, 'Turkish history, you can believe that so many things from the Greeks are a rare offering.' Aliki smiled, remembering the sneer in the voice of the Greek lecturer in the auditorium when referring to Turkish history. The captain continued, 'This is where West and East meet, and for the purpose of understanding the Greek it is good to remember that Greece is very much in the West.'

She studied the momentarily altered expression, but the captain, realising that he had let down a reserve, managed once more the well-tried avuncular look. His intention was to inform and please, free of prejudice, but at the same time to make sure that the passengers left his ship appreciating the glories that were and are Greece. Now he gave confirmation that all was well between them by issuing an invitation to dine with him in a couple of days' time.

Aliki accepted the invitation and together they watched the light-footed approach of Carl Roberts, who, taking the smallest of his cameras from its case, said, 'Say, could I snap our captain here with Mrs Findlay?'

The captain, who had one face for his crew and another for his passengers, now presented yet a third: a glamorous one for the record.

Without waiting for a pose, Carl Roberts snapped and said thanks. He returned the camera to its case, with the surprising neatness and agility she had noticed in all his movements.

He slung the strap of his leather case over his shoulder, as though temporarily dismissing it, and, hooking his arm through Aliki's, said, 'Let's go. The day is getting hotter.'

Over her shoulder Aliki saw her mother comfortably established in a deck chair under a ship's awning and beside her was Mr Fosdick writing on a small pad. '...And a silver bracelet for my god-daughter,' Audrey's voice carried. Mr Fosdick's pen flew efficiently across the page.

Carl Roberts gave a mock salute to the captain as he and Aliki turned to go, and the captain, watching the thin lady and the fat man go, as it were, dancing down the deck, wondered not for the first time what the American's intentions were.

Now, leaving the other passengers to work out their plans for the day, Captain Manoli returned to the bridge and to his day cabin, where there were cables that had to be sorted.

The aura of well-being that seemed to emanate from Carl Roberts came now into the crowded coach. The cool-seeming strength of it stayed with them as the driver hurtled them across red and green lights alike, negotiating with nerve-splitting precision the exit from several crossroads. The coach came to a shrieking standstill outside Istanbul's largest and most famous mosque, and Carl Roberts, unruffled still, said steadily, 'Well, here we are.'

Inside the Blue Mosque, glacial air and blue shadows had for centuries drained off the heat that lay outside the doors. Visitors already in it – dots on a chessboard – carefully trod the many carpets, and Aliki and Carl Roberts, moving further into the great building, recognised passengers who had broken free of tour guides to encapsulate for themselves the quiet, the calm and deep shaded beauty, and to gather fragments of the Koran, *suras*, scattered in sheets here and there. Aliki slipped a few extracts into her bag, and, looking in wonder at the round fluted columns rising as it were to the ceiling, marvelled at their height.

She watched the look of awe on Carl Roberts's face, and doubted if it could be a first experience. He led her to the foot of a single narrow pulpit and pointed to the sign at the bottom: NO ENTRANCE. 'The pulpit waits for the return of the Prophet,' he said.

Soon Elena and Tessa joined them, and slowly they circled the interior, taking deep breaths of the clear air, all amazed by the miracle – perhaps – of a building crowded with people and yet so seemingly empty. Silently they went out through the great doors and into the burning light outside. They picked up their shoes lying in neat rows against the wall and, bending to fasten a sandal, Aliki watched as her mother appeared from out of the mosque, her face wrinkled against the sun but partly protected by the fussing movements of Mr Fosdick, with his sun umbrella. He was now immaculate in a pale-green cotton suit and matching magenta shirt and tie. They joined in the stroll through the gardens that led from the mosque to the more ancient St Sophia, and Aliki, turning to watch the skipping movements of Tessa beside Elena, saw Professor and Frau Friebel emerge from the middle of a group of passengers. The doctor was leaning heavily on his stick.

In front of St Sophia Aliki felt a cold blast go through her. In spite of its renowned elegance she found the great church threatening, and suddenly visions of all the religious wars were conjured up in front of her. Once into the austere interior she shut her eyes to blank out the impressions there and to bring alive the fresco in her cabin where the Minoan goddess walked through scenes of nature, finding epiphany in trees, rocks, birds, flowers. She smiled inwardly at her pagan thinking and stepped once more out into the light.

Around them the short grasses seemed shrivelled by the midday sun, and only here and there a flower stood upright to the rays. Sometimes on the slow walk Elena stopped to touch a wilting shrub and Carl Roberts, leaning towards Aliki, said, 'Ah think they are all coming to a refreshment of life in the numinous presence.'

Aliki felt an area of contentment settle into her head, and watched as Tessa added a skip and a jump to the walk and, finally coming close to the professor, said, 'Is your ideal of beauty Frau Friebel?'

The professor looked pleased, and, turning to regard the ageing, grinning face of his wife and back to the happy young face beside him, said, 'Yes she is. It is by Beauty that beautiful things are beautiful.'

Frau Friebel, putting her hand gently under her husband's elbow, said, 'I think that is enough, dear.'

Mr Fosdick, who had stood silently, turning his head from one speaker to another while holding the sun umbrella over Audrey Martin's head, said, 'I think the coaches will be waiting.' Stretching out a hand towards his new companion, he walked with an authoritative step down the path and led the others back to the waiting coach.

The coach driver, who had plans for his passengers other than those scheduled, took the unsuspecting tourists to his brother's carpet factory down a narrow road hemmed in by a display of flags and hanging clothes. As the passengers filed out of the coach the driver escorted them to the bottom of a dark wooden stairway and pointed to the man waiting at the top.

The stairway opened up into a large room, and the surprised group found themselves contemplating a colourful display of well laid-out rugs. Light from the window focused directly on to them, and soon the swirl of cigarette smoke and fumes of Turkish coffee filled the room. Small white cups of coffee were circling, and those who had at first been annoyed by the deviation entered now into the conspiracy.

Aliki stood at the back of the room beside the only window and watched with a growing feeling of nervousness Audrey's undisguised interest in the carpets. She saw her mother touch and turn them, count stitches and question the men who were hovering over the carpets like fathers with debutante daughters. Around her she could hear comments in Greek, German, Italian and French. Carl Roberts sat two seats away – taking up two seats – and was currently soothing the excited gulps from Tessa.

'But I would just love to take one home for my father,' Tessa said, and Carl Roberts, reaching out to lift the corner of a carpet, said, 'You'd get it at a better price in Harrods, London.'

Aliki shifted her position from the narrow window to the centre of the room where small spotlights beamed on to the carpets, and sat near to Audrey, who was putting in a bid for a sea-green silk. 'I'll give you two hundred pounds.' There was a shocked taking in of breath, and a man at the back of the room, in a guttural voice, called out, 'Two thousand dollars.' The bidding went up and up, and Aliki listened in near panic at the thought that Audrey by her obstinacy might price herself out of the market, until Mr Fosdick, with his new louder voice, took the bidding out of her mother's reach to the point where only a German and a Greek were left competing. She looked at her mother's small companion, now seated comfortably in his chair, and saw a fundamental change in the man. The apologetic, almost self-deprecating air had been replaced by one of protective concern and, as his eyes went from one bidder to another, his glance now and again dropped to watch the woman beside him. How had she failed to notice that the small moustache, which had rested so uneasily on his lip, had gone, and the long upper lip had become now the main feature of his face? She laughed briefly and the sound of it, cancelling the atmosphere of tension in the room, brought dealings to a conclusion.

The impetus that had propelled the coachload of passengers up the creaking narrow staircase now had them filing out through the door and back down the steps. Once into the light, Aliki saw Elena standing in the doorway opposite, smiling and pointing to a bundle under her arm. 'Carl said I could buy this for Tessa to take home to Canada for her father. It's nearer the true price.' Audrey turned to Mr Fosdick. 'Were you pricing me out of the bidding on purpose?'

'Er ... yes.' He smiled, the long upper lip moving with caution over his top teeth, the beaming pleasure of the man suddenly there for all to see. He stooped to pick up the carpet, which Elena had spread on the pavement, and, examining it, said, 'Now you really have a bargain.'

From her front seat position inside the coach, Aliki turned to see if the professor and his wife were still with them.

'Have we left the Germans behind?'

'Ah saw them call a cab outside the gardens. Maybe the professor was having trouble with his leg.'

The coach driver had a different attitude now; money had been got out of the passengers, the day was getting hotter and the journey to the ship was made without any detours.

Once on board, each passenger returned his landing-disc to the metal sheet on A Deck, and Carl Roberts, pointing to three gaps on it, said, 'The Millers are still at large in Istanbul.' He looked at his watch. 'It's close on sailing time.'

In fact, Peter Miller was sitting beside the driver of a taxi-cab, telling the man the route back to the ship, and at the same time trying to silence the accusation from behind.

'For God's sake, Peter, leave the man alone. And stop breathing alcohol all over him,' Daphne Miller called out.

'If you were sitting where I am,' Peter Miller countered, 'you'd be worrying about the smell of garlic, not booze.'

'Why we had to go to the Hilton for lunch I'll never understand. It was bound to take ages to be served.'

'I couldn't invite Jonathan Rivers to any old dump,' Peter Miller said, and, leaning across the driver, took hold of the steering wheel and swerved it to the right. The driver jammed his foot on the brake, stopped the car, got out, went round to the other side of the cab and, pushing his head in through the passenger window, let out a torrent of words that ended with something that sounded like, 'You drive.'

Peter Miller slid across to the driving seat, yelled at the driver, 'Well, get in, can't you,' and revved the engine.

By the time the authorities on board had noticed the three missing discs, Major and Mrs Miller, Miss Wainwright and their irate driver had already twice circled the eastern and more ancient part of Istanbul and were now at last heading for the quay.

'Christ, I know our ship's here somewhere,' Peter Miller was saying to himself, and the driver, who had given up shouting and had now taken to hitting his customer, managed at last the imperative word, 'Halt'. Responding to the ancient word of command, the Major brought the car to a standstill under the stern of the *Laconia*.

'All right. What's the charge?'

Pointing to the wad of notes in the Englishman's hand, the driver indicated that the whole amount would about cover it, and Daphne Miller, leaping from the car, said, 'Give it to him.'

'Like hell I will.' Peter Miller stood on the quay counting and muttering something about 'who had driven the bloody thing anyway'. Handing over a few notes, he followed his women up the gangway. 'I hope we never have to return to this God-forsaken place,' he said, stuffing his wallet into the back pocket of his trousers.

'Good evening, Major Miller.' The captain had come down to greet the wandering members of his flock, and was even considering the Major with added insight. 'I trust you have had a pleasant day in the colourful city of Istanbul.' He looked down into the anxiously smiling, upturned face of Daphne Miller and said, 'I see your husband has bought you each a present.' Similar silver necklaces adorned the bronzed throats of the two women.

'It beats me what the women see in these hot, fly-infested bazaars.'

'Poor Peter had to take us to the Hilton to cool off,' Daphne Miller beamed at the captain, and Molly Wainwright, dabbing at the small beads of sweat on her forehead, and as if in vindication of their expensive lunch, said, 'To meet the British Consul.'

'Old friend of mine, old boy. At school together, you know. Funny thing is he's gone native ever since. Can't make head or tail of his obsession with the lazy sods. You should have seen the condition of some of the back streets, I mean ...'

The captain had seen the condition of the streets many a time. The idea of glamour had gone from the city of Istanbul voyages ago, the present apparently increasing inertia of the Turk a further cause for amazement that invasion of his country had ever taken place.

'You will enjoy the amenities of the ship all the more.' He smiled sweetly at the Major and made a silent vow to reprimand him, when he should be in a more receptive mood, about keeping the entire schedule waiting. And perhaps on the last night of the cruise, the game of choosing 'Mr Laconia' – the most popular man on the ship – could be set against Major Miller. It would be amusing to embarrass the Englishman a little.

'Tomorrow we arrive in Patmos,' he called to the departing back, and the Major, turning round, said, 'What I need is a drink.'

Two decks above, as Peter Miller made for the whisky bottle in his cabin, Carl Roberts and Aliki, who had witnessed the sensational arrival of the Millers on to the ship, sat now together in a cool corner of the Verandah Deck lounge, sipping iced Coca-Cola and for the moment saying nothing.

Then: 'It was kind of you to give Tessa that rug,' Aliki spoke finally and pushed at the floating pieces of ice in her drink.

Carl Roberts, who was sitting well back in his chair, one leg resting on another said, 'Did you see the kid's face?' He uncrossed his legs and leant forward.

'Who's the woman with her?'

'I don't know. She's never around for us to find out. Have you noticed how good Elena is with Tessa?'

'Elena can recognise a cry for help when she hears one.'

He leant back, smiled and said, 'Ah enjoyed the Major's arrival. Does the guy do it on purpose, d'you reckon?'

'I think he is what he is. I'm not surprised there have to be two women. One couldn't cope.'

'He does all right.' Carl Roberts put down his glass and, looking at the woman beside him, said, 'Okay, honey, so he has two women, your mother now seems to have Mr Fosdick, the Germans have each other, Elena has, well, she has everyone, but what about you?'

A lump of ice that was in Aliki's mouth went down her throat in a spasm. She waited for the feeling of coldness to pass. 'Actually, I don't need anyone.'

Carl Roberts got up from his chair, slid some money over the bar counter and said to Costas, 'Another iced coke, please, and a double whisky.' He moved back to the table with a glass in each hand and shoved the whisky towards Aliki. 'Tell me more.'

The rush of tears to her eyes was stopped by the sight of Peter Miller bearing down on them. He sat close, his head turning from one to the other. 'Bloody daylight robbery.' His arm swept backwards. 'If they're going to charge those prices they might at least clean the place up. Litter everywhere. I've nearly bought both the Hilton and the taxi service attached. He looked towards the bar and bawled out, 'George!' He pulled a packet of cigarettes out of his jacket pocket and, dropping them on the floor, displayed his state of mind.

Costas, who had observed the behaviour of the volatile Englishman, had also known from the man's first appearance in the bar that he would be seeing quite a lot of him. At first he had responded to the name 'George' and even been quite pleased to be compared to a barman in an English club. Now he resented the impersonal mode of address.

Carl Roberts turned in his chair and addressed Costas. 'Bring the Major a vodka and tonic, please, Costas.'

'The girls are in the hairdressers' getting cleaned up.' Peter Miller drew deeply on his cigarette and lowered his other arm.

'I thought the Blue Mosque was one of the most peaceful buildings I have ever been in.' Aliki hoped to retrieve something from their visit to Istanbul, but Peter Miller, staring at the space between them as if Aliki's words might contaminate the air, said simply, 'Muslims!'

Costas arrived with the vodka and tonic and stood above the Major holding the tray, and Carl Roberts, looking up, said, 'Put it on my bill, please, Costas.'

The Major drank, the vodka settling nicely on top of the whisky he had consumed in his cabin, and an exhausted mellowness took over. He sank back into his chair, nodded a little, and Carl Roberts and Aliki resumed their conversation but no longer, as before, on the personal note.

Aliki got up suddenly. 'I don't want to miss the lecture on Patmos and Rhodes.' She thanked Carl Roberts for the drinks and, nodding to Peter Miller, walked quickly towards the interior stairway.

She knew that she was already late for the lecture but an idea had come to her suddenly. It formed in her mind as she went down the stairs: she would give a drinks party in her cabin in order to entertain a few of the ship's officers. From one of them, she hoped, she would get information about her early morning and late evening deck contact. She bumped into two smiling Americans on the stairs and wondered whether to invite them. At the bottom was the beady-eyed chief purser, and he, she felt certain, would know.

She said, 'I'm having a few people for drinks in my cabin tomorrow evening. Can you come?' The officer consulted his memory. 'Yes. Thank you.'

'Eight o'clock,' she said.

Inside her cabin, and with the lights dimmed, Aliki sat in front of the dressing-table staring at her reflection. Carl Roberts had underlined a truth: almost everyone on board was with someone. She had even written to the shipping office for a cabin far from her mother. Why? She tried a different expression on her face: one of determination. When the cruise was nearly over she would tell Audrey that she was going to find a flat of her own.

There was a knock on the door and Nikos walked in.

'You want something?' He pointed to the light outside the door and Aliki, looking up, said, 'Can you press this for tonight?' She held up a crumpled dress.

Nikos look at his watch. 'Is late.'

'I know it's too late for dinner, but I want it for later.'

Nikos stared straight through the porthole, his expression changing to one of benign understanding. 'So,' he said, 'a rendezvous.' The French expression came clumsily off his tongue, but formalised what was in Aliki's mind and made even louder her protest of 'Certainly not'. Nikos turned and, surprised by the dismissive tone, lifted the dress. 'I iron it good.'

He walked quickly out of the cabin.

The voices in the cabin forward were surprisingly high-toned. Perhaps the Italian couple had got off the cruise at Istanbul and had now been replaced. She had never seen her neighbours except on the night of the Roman party when she had caught a glimpse of them disappearing down the passageway, laurel leaves – or some such – on their heads, their bodies swathed in sheets. She had enjoyed the giggles from this elderly couple who rose late in the mornings and led quite a night bar life. She was aware that through the day people drifted this way and that, some faces becoming more familiar than others. Any inclination to wander from their own group was nipped at the source by the divisions passengers had already made. The city–states of Classical Greece had now been realised in the self-imposed ethnic barriers. She would like to expand their unit slightly. Molecules viewed under the microscope could not behave with more predictability than the different accumulative cells here on board. Captain Manoli could be the Flying Dutchman for all he would ever reach a safe harbour and his dream of overall unity.

The couple next door might be Greek. She was beginning to recognise the sounds. Doctor Friebel, comparing the Greek of classical times with modern Greek, said there was a restlessness about the latter because artistic expression was no longer there. She regretted now that she had turned down the captain's invitation for dinner and wondered how soon she could silence the rumblings in her stomach. Trickery from the carpet-interested coach-driver had left them all without lunch.

She turned to face the cabin aft. For the last two nights the voices in there had been silent. Had Nikos found another cabin for Tessa? Or was there – thanks to Elena – peace between the two?

She pulled her book from the bedside table. She would study the Minoan figures once more, particularly the faces of the young men, and see if she could relate them to the man on the deck.

'Come in.' Nikos's knock was more a gesture of arrival than a request to enter. Now he stood in the cabin holding up her dress.

'You've done it beautifully,' she said.

'Is cold on deck tonight. Keep it for when the moon shines.'

Aliki laughed. 'It is very un-Greek of you to be so romantic.' But Nikos, putting the dress on a hanger, ignored the remark. He knew what he knew.

She said, 'What has happened to the lady next door?'

Nikos looked surprised. 'You not know?'

'No.'

'Is sick. In hospital.'

'Perhaps it's the best place for her.' She smiled at Nikos.

'Is very sick. Daughter should be with her now.'

'What did you say?'

'Is daughter. That lady is mother.'

She stared at Nikos, who stared back. So she had been right. What crazy game had Tessa been playing?

'You go and see.'

Aliki noticed the change of atmosphere from her last visit. In place of the welcoming salon there was now the dedicated silence of the sick room. The doctor and the nurse were one on either side of the bed of the sick woman, whose complexion was a pale yellow. She lay with her eyes shut, her arm attached to a drip, and a tube was coming out the bottom of the bed. Aliki, remembering the occasion when Tessa had been similarly connected, saw now the real illness.

'I have sent Tessa to take a shower.' The doctor spoke over his shoulder as he tested the bottle hanging above the woman's head. 'She came in from Istanbul without changing her clothes.'

'Oh, then I ...' Aliki took a step backwards and the doctor said, 'Please, you also.'

From the door she said, 'Is there anything I can do?'

'Make sure the girl comes. Until now she has not accepted the illness. My patient needs her.'

Aliki hesitated. 'How long have you known of this illness?'

'Yesterday. The lady collapse.'

'You mean …?'

'Please.' The doctor took the fresh bottle of saline drip from the nurse and fixed it on the stand. He said, 'Later we can talk.' He turned to look at Aliki. 'Persuade the girl to come.'

Walking down the passageway from the hospital, she wondered what craziness had driven Tessa to bring all attention on herself. How could anger against a dying mother lead to such a charade? Was it … was it perhaps the only way she could cope with the visible deterioration of a beloved … friend? She still had difficulty accepting that the woman might be the girl's mother.

Her knock on the cabin door brought Tessa's voice faintly to her, and, walking into the room, she saw that Tessa was on the bunk with her back to the porthole and Elena on the other one facing her. Tessa's face was strained and white, but tearless.

She said, 'He wants me back in there, doesn't he?'

Hesitating momentarily, Aliki sat on the bed beside her. 'Your … mother…,' she began, but Tessa, interrupting, said, 'I was telling Elena about the car accident.'

She took hold of the silver bracelet on Aliki's wrist and began to twist. 'My father was a racing-driver and occasionally he would take me for a spin.'

'Yes?'

'I loved it. My mother hated it, but came.' She twisted the bracelet the other way and Aliki sucked in her breath. 'One day, he thought he would try out a new gear change on a sharp bend, and …'

'What age were you?'

'Nine. And the car, instead of responding properly, shot across the road, went up a bank and tumbled into a small quarry.' Tessa shut her eyes and, Aliki, taking the girl's hand off her bracelet, held on to it. 'I was thrown clear of the wreck,' Tessa continued, 'and was bounced into some bushes. My mother and father were crushed by the shattered vehicle, and a few hours later died in hospital.'

Aliki felt the grip on her hand and, looking deeply into the memory of it all in Tessa's eyes, thought how both their fathers had died from a form of bravado. She studied the small scar on the girl's chin and, reaching out her other hand, touched it gently.

'The person in the hospital bed is my foster mother, and I don't want to go in there and watch her die.'

'Doctor Anagnosti could cure her.' Aliki was trying to absorb the new information.

Elena crossed the space between the two bunks and, taking hold of Tessa's other hand, opened the clenched fingers. She said, 'Accidents, Tessa, are by accident. They are not planned.' She looked for confirmation from Aliki, who sat now with her eyes shut, deep in her own vicarious experience of her father's accident. She was with him on the horse, travelling against the rush of the wind. Lifting ... lifting over the gate, misjudging the landing, Aliki's scream splintering the air – or was it her father's scream? – she landing in the soft grass, her father not getting up again from under the horse.

She shook her head, looked directly at Tessa, and said, 'I also lost my father in an accident, but this was on a horse.'

'How terrible!' Tessa took both of Aliki's hands in hers. 'How really terrible. But you have your mother. Mine, I mean, my foster-mother has come on this cruise to die. Actually to die.' Tessa's voice broke, then, continuing, said, 'She wanted so much to see Greece and the islands. My foster father said, "Take her". But you see she has been too ill to go anywhere, do anything. And I have been behaving ...'

'You are fond of your foster mother, aren't you?' Elena said.

'I love her.'

'Well, then,' Elena stood up and went to hold open the door, 'prove it to her by going in there.'

'Come on,' Aliki said suddenly, and stretched an arm out towards Tessa. 'I think we ought to give the doctor all the support we can.'

Down the passageway they ran into Nikos, and Tessa, catching hold of the lapels of his white jacket, said: 'Please Nikos, come with us to the hospital.'

Nikos backed against the wall, his hands to it. 'Is good you go. I see you later.' He gave a hesitant grin and, looking at Aliki as if he would praise her for her attendance on the girl, hurried down the passageway.

Tessa's footsteps began to drag and Aliki said, 'Listen, when we have visited your mother we'll have dinner together, and then we'll go for a swim in the moonlight.'

'Oh, let's.' The child in Tessa was now uppermost, and

with more of a spring in her step she went with Aliki down the stairway to B Deck and into the hospital.

Inside the hospital soft lights and the smell of sweetly scented soap and body powder told that the patient had been settled for the night. The doctor was no longer in the room and the night nurse sat making up a chart in the anteroom. Mrs McAllister lay as before with her eyes shut, but there was a calm now about the recumbent figure. Opening her eyes and seeing movement by the door, and then recognising Tessa, she gave a faint smile. Tessa leaped across the room and, kneeling by the bed, put her head down on it. A thin hand caressed her hair.

Aliki stood breathing quietly, then moving on tiptoe to the locker by Mrs McAllister's bed, picked up the mother-of-pearl Bible resting there. In the anteroom she said to the nurse, 'Please tell Doctor Anagnosti that I am borrowing this for a day.'

'Who is this that darkeneth counsel by words without knowledge?' Aliki sat on the Sun Deck whispering the words to herself, her head bent to the mother-of-pearl Bible. And further into *Job* she read, 'Where wast thou when I laid the foundations of the earth?'

Where indeed?

'Hast thou commanded the morning since thy days? And caused the dayspring to know its place?'

She closed the Bible and looked across the deck at the approaching island of Patmos. The monastery of St John the Divine was casting a huge shadow over the land. She would not go ashore today. The island commanded no greater view of the Aegean Sea than did her viewpoint here, actually a part of the sea, and certainly – at the point of horizon – in touch with the sky. She knew now that the impact of this area was with her not only during the day but also in her dreams. Since the start of the sail round the southern islands, their stark beauty and the supporting light had penetrated to the part of the brain where lasting record is made. The islands, both close and far, coming into view, seemed like stepping-stones, one to another, a harmony of brown hill, deep blue sky and indigo sea. Even her interest in going ashore, getting her feet actually on land, was becoming diminished by this almost celestial view of ... Creation.

As the ship came slowly to anchor she dug into her canvas bag and brought out some sheets of *suras* from the Koran, found in the Blue Mosque. At the same time she opened the Bible and began to compare tracts from both.

From the New Testament, St John, she read out loud, 'And I saw a new heaven and a new earth, for the first heaven and the first earth were passed away, and there was no more sea.' She looked around her quizzically. From the Koran, speaking now with deeper tone, she spoke out the words, 'When the sun is folded up, And when the stars fall. And when the seas shall boil … then …' Then what? *Sura* 84: 'When the heaven shall have split asunder and duteously obeys its Lord; And when the Earth shall have been stretched out as a plain. And shall have cast forth what was in her and become empty. Then verily, Oh Man, who desirest to reach thy Lord, shalt thou meet him.'

'I see.' She read further from St John. 'There shall be no more death, neither sorrow, nor crying, neither shall there be any more pain.'

'The two Books seem to be agreed, and the creation of Man can be forgotten forever.'

'Good afternoon, Mrs Findlay, are we not going ashore today?' The captain had appeared over her right shoulder, and, irritated, Aliki hid the Bible and the tracts from Islam under her towel.

'I'll hear about it from the others,' she answered, and was surprised to find the captain taking her statement personally.

'Are you still … um … off-colour?' He seemed momentarily pleased with the colloquialism, but frowned again. 'Perhaps the food is still not to your liking?'

'It's nothing to do with food. I don't like monasteries or convents or churches or mosques.' She spread her arms around as if to embrace the scene around her and, looking up at the captain, added, 'And I like them even less in the company of a lot of jostling, pushing sightseers.'

Captain Manoli stood to attention. 'We try on board this ship to give the impression of space around the individual.'

He was used to passengers making complaints that attention was not personal enough. In spite of the three hundred others on board, each wanted, because he had paid for it, the feeling that he was on an exclusive voyage. What he had not expected was that Mrs Findlay would show both disappointment and temperament, enough perhaps to upset the balance of behaviour on the ship.

He tried a safe question: 'And what about Mrs Martin, is she going ashore today?'

Aliki thought of the early morning when she'd been swimming in the indoor pool. Audrey and Mr Fosdick had come in. Audrey was wearing a clinging bathing suit, and beside her Mr Fosdick – a rainbow of colour – was in a striped dressing-gown revealing a pair of trunks of small proportions. At first the couple had not seen the figure in the pool and, going to their respective shower rooms, had come out wet and shivering with anticipation. Each ventured in a toe.

'Good morning, Audrey,' Aliki said, and the foot that shot out of the water nearly hit her on the head.

'What are you doing here?'

'Swimming.'

They had all swum together, Mr Fosdick making little blowing noises as he paddled rapidly backwards and forwards, her mother's progress more stately as she went from one side to the other, and Aliki, attempting a dive in imitation of Elena, found herself swimming underwater with a certain feeling of discovery. When Audrey came up out of the water, Mr Fosdick was attentive with an open towel and, watching the gesture, Aliki lay in the water studying the small man as he stood firmly on the side of the pool. Exposure to the Aegean air was giving a golden firmness to his body, and the admiration that shone from his eyes when he looked at her mother seemed to confirm his developing confidence. She wondered if it was possible that this was the sort of uncomplicated attention that her mother had been seeking over the years. It seemed paradoxical that such an attitude should be realised in such a naturally diffident man.

'Sorry. What did you say?' Aliki realised that the captain was waiting for an answer.

He repeated, 'Your mother, is she going ashore today?'

'My mother will go ashore at Rhodes where there are shops to explore. She is not interested in ruins and …'

'Greek history?'

Captain Manoli turned to go and Aliki, holding up an arm, said, 'Will you be coming to my drinks party this evening?'

The captain revolved on one foot. 'Forgive the oversight. I have already written to accept.'

'Good.' Watching him stride down the deck, she remembered how he had looked the day she had seen him off-duty in civilian clothes. Then he had been all smiles and relaxation. But this was a ship, the finest of its kind, and he was responsible for everyone on it.

Leaning over the rails and watching disembarkation into the tenders, she saw that her mother *was* going ashore today, and that Mr Fosdick, the Major and his two women, were with her. Conversation among them seemed easy and fluid.

She walked about on the deck. Was Audrey interested in Greek history? Her mother seemed quite pleased with her mixed blood of Greek and Irish, but Aliki doubted if she gave the history of either much thought. Discussion between them had always been about matters of the moment. She didn't think Audrey carried around with her thoughts that delved into the reason for behaviour. The effect of habit had managed to produce between them the same result as the effect of affection. There was an awareness between them that almost certainly had nothing to do with love.

Now, as she watched the tenders make for the small port, where sailing craft were on the shore like sweets scattered from a box of licorice all-sorts, she stood watching the scramble for the single coach. She kept her eyes on the bus interior as the passengers climbed aboard, and there was the Major, standing beside the driver. Could it be to show him the way?

Turning her chair east, to face the coast of Asia Minor, she sank back into it, at the same time lifting a book from the bottom of her bag, the book tracing the development of Islam from the seventh century to the present time. She gave a short laugh. Did she think she could absorb all of that in one sitting? But looking at a picture of the Dome of the Rock in Jerusalem, she nodded as she read, 'the *mythoi* of religion are not like the demonstrable facts of science.' And yet ... and yet, here in front of her was the demonstration of the insights of art. Now that she came to think of it, why had she not paid more attention to the exterior of the great mosque in Istanbul, instead of a reserving her fascination for the strangely earthbound aestheticism of the interior.

'Hi.' It was Carl Roberts. He had come looking for her, from deck to deck.

She sat up. 'Aren't you going to visit the island?'

'Ah've been and Ah'm back.'

How long had she been here, she wondered. She looked at her watch. What did she do with the hours? A soft, almost peach light was around them.

'How was the monastery?'

'Ah never got that far.'

'Oh!'

'The crowds! You have a better view of it here.' He dragged a chair close to hers. Lowering himself into it, and pulling down his hat against the diamond-shafting evening sun, he said, 'Have you thought if you'd like to see me in London?'

The vision she had of him suddenly was of a large figure in the centre of London squeezed into a dark suit and tipping doormen. She laughed, and he said, 'You don't do that often.'

He leaned closer, 'Are you going to see me in London?'

This time her vision was of the large, kind face, shrewd, amused eyes, freckled, hairy hands negotiating her through crowds into expensive, exclusive places.

'*If* I go there.'

'How's that?'

'I'm planning to get a place of my own. It may not be in England.'

'The world's a small place, honey, for people of mah wealth.' He grinned.

She turned to look fully at him. 'If I were to tell you that I've met a man on this ship who only ever appears in the dark, would you believe me?'

'Ah'd say he was a fool.'

'A fool?'

'You look great in sunlight.'

'Seriously, though. You might have seen me talking to him during our early morning arrival in Istanbul.'

Carl Roberts pushed his hat back. 'It was the darnedest thing seeing you up that early.'

'But, Carl, did you see me talking to this small Greek? I think he was Greek.'

'Is this the same guy who didn't exist in the streets of Mykonos?'

She collapsed into her chair. Did it matter that she have confirmation that someone else had seen him? She looked into the laughing kind eyes and wondered if it was a look of tenderness she saw in there. She said, 'Are you and Elena … I mean … is there some sort of …?'

'It's simple. Her playing gives me some sort of happiness, and my feeling of happiness gives substance to her playing.' He covered her hand with his large one. 'You can't spend the rest of your life on your own.'

'But I …'

'Yeah?'

'I have difficulty with involvement.'

'I gave up this sort of discussion at university,' he said and, pointing to his frame, added, 'and built this comfortable vehicle inside which to propel myself.'

'I've never built anything,' she said with emphasis, and then wondered if she should tell him what the old witch in Ireland had told her about Fate ruling her life. Instead she tried, 'Is the modern-day Cretan in any way connected with the men of the Minoan civilisation of long ago?' She looked at him out of the corner of her eye, and he, responding as she thought he would, said, 'It's that guy again, isn't it? That weirdo who floats about in the dark, dropping in and out of the centuries.'

'I know its not possible, but on the other hand ...'

'You're seeing him?'

'I might as well tell you that there is a fresco in my cabin, a beautiful picture of the Minoan people wandering about in a garden. They are small, compact, handsome, and...' she was watching his expression, and trying to control her enthusiasm for the subject, '... and the book I am in reading in my cabin, The *Dawn of Civilisation*, says that the Minoan civilisation was based on a worship of the beautiful in nature, of living matter, of the earth goddess ...' She averted her eyes from his gaze, '... And the people come alive in my cabin.'

'Yeah. Well, the captain will encourage all that sort of thing. It sells cruises.'

'But surely ...'

'Most civilisations started with a worship of nature, which

became a cult of the dead or dying.' He leaned forward again, his large frame tightening suddenly. 'It was Ancient Greece that was able to convert the Minoan unproductive cult of the dead into something vital.'

She stood up. Was it anger she felt? 'The Minoan was one of the most advanced and gracious civilisations the world has ever known,' she protested.

He stretched out a hand and pulled her into the chair. 'That too. But those palaces you'll have been reading about, hot and cold running water, were all for the dead. The Minoans were not taken to the world of the hereafter in imagination alone. They and their families were literally conducted into the underworld of funerary caves and palaces.'

'Knossos?'

He nodded.

'But it's in the history books that...'

'Ah ...liki,' he spun out the name, 'do you see those athletic little girls in your fresco, leaping over bulls' heads?'

'Sometimes.'

'Well, they're not doing it for fun.'

'Athletics and dancing were part of ...'

'... the sacrifice to the earth goddess.'

They sat in silence, watching the sunset pattern the sky. Was she relieved to have the whole myth exploded, or appalled at her own near attempt to be a part of the death cult?

'And listen, honey,' Carl Roberts broke the silence, watching her carefully, 'the Spanish told Sir Arthur Evans that leaping over a savage bull by a girl is impossible. The bull's horns penetrated the girl's chest. That was part of the sacrifice.' She noticed that the Southern drawl was crisper, his mind more engaged. He continued, 'You for some reason want, or perhaps wanted, to believe that four thousand years ago there was a civilisation greater than our own, and that outside influences brought it to extinction. Crushed perhaps by a volcanic eruption. Or sunk into the sea.'

'Well, didn't it? At least physically?'

'I guess you prefer to see it that way. A glorious death for a people who brought beauty into dying.' He was looking at her carefully, studying her, she thought. He said, 'Is that what goes on up there on deck – a search for a death companion?'

'Everything in our religion is to do with sacrifice and death. The crucifixion, St John of the Cross, Communion.'

'But there is also resurrection. And not only the Christians thought of that.'

She could sense the rarely glimpsed Carl Roberts, and listened carefully.

'Thirty-five hundred years ago a new way of thinking actually germinated in Crete: a resurrection of ideas following sacrifice.'

'But …'

'Thanks to the Greeks they were able to escape from a fundamentally Stone Age religion towards a life of the mind.'

Does he really know? Does anyone?

She watched him formulating, and he continued, 'Your history books will tell you that the Minoan civilisation became the Mycenaean, which in turn became the Hellenic, and from the Hellenic – so it seems – came the humanistic principles of education, exercise of language and, of course, expansion of the mind.'

She realised he was grinning at her and she grinned back.

'Don't just take the word of some fat American, check it out.'

Rising lightly out of his chair and stretching out a hand, he said, 'What we need is a drink.'

She saw that the benign playboy was back. He was returning to the role that would make the rest of the journey comfortable for them both.

As if by silent communication, Elena appeared on deck. She walked towards them, discarding her clothes and pinning her hair on top of her head.

'Come for a swim.'

'Don't tell me, honey, that you made it to the monastery?'

She dived into the water and surfaced. 'You are talking to a seasoned continental traveller who has learnt to use both elbows and feet when it comes to coping with queues.' She laughed and others, hearing the sound, gathered round.

Elena spread her towel on the deck beside Aliki, Aliki making room for her and watching the water bubbles pop all over her body in a sunset pink of effusion, the radiation coming from both woman and sun, she thought.

Lifting herself on an elbow, Elena said, 'Tessa has gone for another visit to the hospital. I do not think you and I will be needed there any more.'

'But she's fun to have around,' Aliki said emphatically, and Elena, rising on an elbow, said, 'For the moment she has work to do.'

Studying her now, Aliki said, 'You are actually more Greek than Italian, aren't you?'

'I'm completely Greek. Through and through. Back and back. It was my husband who gave me the wonderful surname d'Capatorre.'

Carl Roberts had dropped back in his chair and was admiring the women close to him, as they were wondering how much longer the canvas would hold as the congenial bulk heaved itself in and out.

'D'you think the visit to Crete tomorrow will invite a reliving of the Major's wartime experiences?' Aliki twinkled at them, including in her glance others gathered round. 'Daphne Miller insists we've got it coming.'

'Y'all ah hard on that guy, and ah don't think he deserves it.'

'How naive you are, Carl. He has been inviting tauntings from me since we came on board,' Elena said.

'With those two women like putty in his hands he needs something knobbly to chew on. Besahdes, Ah've an idea he's the odd one out in that threesome.'

Audrey and Mr Fosdick appeared now, walking briskly round the deck, stepping in time. Aliki followed the movement, her eyes wide open.

Carl Roberts, looking towards Aliki, said, 'Something's happened to that guy,' and Aliki, watching the couple turn on the deck, surprised herself with, 'I like him.'

'I've decided to visit the palace of Knossos tomorrow even if there is a crowd,' Elena said. 'And you, Carl? You do not come often enough off the ship. Will you come tomorrow, chéri?' She stretched out her arms as if to make the offer of a palace.

'Ah reckon Ah'll be staying on board tomorrow. There are things Ah've to attend to.'

'Carl is telephoning every morning to his office in Houston. Picture that.'

Aliki pictured it, and as the vision of the large man seated by the telephone in the stateroom came to her, there came with it the idea of him as someone of influence and power. She turned towards him, as if to see the mark of decision-making there, but his face in repose was relaxed and yielding and different again from the expression when talking about ancient civilisations.

Once more Audrey and Mr Fosdick circled the deck, and this time, as they passed, Aliki called out, 'Hello.' Startled, the two hesitated, looked, smiled and without losing speed went on their way.

She watched them collide with the more stately progress of Professor and Frau Friebel circling the deck, slowly, the other way, the professor heavy on his stick. 'There goes a true scholar,' Carl Roberts said. 'He never talks unless he has something to contribute.'

'If I hurry, I'll be in time for the captain's lecture on Crete.' Aliki looked at her watch. 'Too late,' she said. 'See you all for drinks in my cabin around eight.'

Entering her cabin, she undressed and went into the shower. Already she could feel some of Carl Roberts's words seeping into her. Shedding a shell, she thought.

An hour later there was a brief tap on the door, and the door opened. Nikos stood there in clean tunic, a tray of glasses balanced on one hand and a white tea towel over his shoulders. He pushed a pair of shoes under the bed and set the tray on top of it.

'Leave the tidying to me,' Aliki said. 'If you get the ice, I'll sort the room.' She stepped into the green and white kaftan, the least crumpled of her two dresses, and was ready for the chief purser, who at eight o'clock knocked on the door. The crispness of his white uniform was in stark contrast to the multiple colours arrayed on her other guests standing close behind him.

'Good evening, Mr Kondomanolio.'

'Good evening.'

'Hello.'

'Hi.'

The guests filed in, dressed, she felt, for an occasion that overlaid the existing atmosphere of an Aegean night and wearing the slightly self-conscious smile that comes when a new mood is being sought. That most of her guests spent the day together, in one activity or another, had nothing to do with the present greetings.

'Whisky and soda?'

'White wine, please.'

'Vodka and tonic?'

'On the rocks.'

Nikos swivelled back into the room, a bowl of ice in one hand, several bottles of tonic and soda water grasped in the other.

Professor and Frau Friebel were the last to arrive and, greeting them by the door, Aliki complimented them on their fresh-looking appearance and asked if the bus ride to the monastery had spoilt the outing.

'No. No. The monastery is magnificent.'

'Very holy, I expect.' She wondered if she was developing a light-hearted attitude to religion.

She led the professor across the cabin to the only chair and he, smiling, said, 'Thank you, no. Tonight I am bringing my strong stick.' He leaned on it and turned to Elena, she, nearly his height, standing face to face with him. The professor kept his eyes averted from the plunging neckline, and asked her about Tessa's mother.

'Doctor Anagnosti is working some sort of miracle with her. He has understanding of more than just the body.'

'You have met him?'

'Yes. After I am falling on the stairs.'

Moving with difficulty across the crowding cabin, Aliki brought with her the captain, Major and Mrs Miller and Molly Wainwright.

'Professor Friebel, I don't know if you have had a chance to talk to the captain.'

'Good evening.'

'Good evening. I have had the pleasure to dine at his table.'

The professor shook hands formally and Peter Miller, standing close to Nikos, who was supporting a tray of drinks, said, 'It's a bit late for introductions, isn't it?' He lifted a couple of glasses off the tray and addressed the captain. 'Everything sorted out on the trip, eh? The Krauts over their paranoia?'

Daphne Miller and Molly Wainwright exchanged hurried glances and studied the expression on both the professor's and Frau Friebel's faces. Slowly Captain Manoli turned from Major Miller and, lifting his glass towards Aliki, said, 'To our charming hostess. May we have many sailings together.'

Forcing his way through, as if in the circumstances space must be expandable, Nikos poured into the glasses, dropped in ice and went from guest to guest to the accompaniment of a slightly off-key hum.

'Say, do you think you could get me an iced Coke?' Carl Roberts walked in from his position by the porthole and Aliki, stretching out a hand to him at the same moment of making an introduction between Mr Kondomanolio and Frau Friebel, said, 'I'm so sorry.'

'Don't apologise, honey. Ah've got all the time in the world.' The crooked grin, which she'd not seen lately, slid up the side of his face and, she, reaching over, kissed him on the cheek.

'Ahm Ah not the privileged one?' He returned the kiss and holding out his hand accepted a glass from Nikos. 'Thanks,' he said and then, looking across the cabin, 'Some guy has just come into the room.'

Mr Manalokas, the chief engineer, had crept silently into the room and was standing by himself just inside the door, his eyes on Elena who was moving towards him. Aliki saw the look both of relief and recognition in his face and, studying the expression, wondered how often Elena sailed these seas. She joined him by the door, shook hands with him, and the contact reminded her of the rhythmic dance they had shared one evening. His smile was polite but distant; he had the distracted look of one who is listening for something. Could it be that the pulsating of the engines – their accurate rhythm – might always be in the mind of the ship's chief engineer?

'Are things going well?' she asked, not knowing the right terms to be used in the circumstances. She realised how little thought she had given to the actual running of the ship. Activity below was of so little interest to them all; the frenzied paddling of the feet of the swan was best left unconsidered.

'Going well?' the chief engineer queried, and Elena, stretching her hand to touch the man, said, 'She means it has been a beautifully smooth cruise.' The words came out of her mouth in the same curving caress as the movement of her arm, and Mr Manalokas, who never listened to flattery from the passengers, allowed now this seduction to reach him. He bowed. 'I thank you.'

Daphne Miller and Molly Wainwright came awkwardly across the room, their glasses raised above their heads, and the chief engineer, seeing the same expression on two different faces, tried to think if he had danced with either woman.

He nodded a greeting and Mrs Miller, throwing her head back, said, 'Isn't this fun?' She turned to see if Peter, for whom she had accepted the invitation, had found yet the hard centre of the party. She smiled to herself when she saw that he was currently basking in the feline presence of the Greek woman.

After a time voices were pitched higher, possibly words more meaningless and, sensing a mood of departure, Aliki wondered if now would be the time to talk privately to Mr Kondomanolio, the chief purser. She eased her way towards him, but Professor Friebel, whose twitching leg was to be the actual catalyst for departure, took hold of her hand in both of his and, talking with a new intimacy, said, 'Such a lovely prelude to our visit to Crete.'

'We thank you.' Frau Friebel's head nodded vigorously.

'Goodbye.'

'Goodbye,' Aliki said warmly. In a few minutes she would see them all again in the dining room.

'Well, I expect we ought to be going,' Carl Roberts called across the cabin to Elena, and she, with her hand propped against the wall above the chief engineer's head, answered, 'I will join you at the table in a little while, chéri.' Mr Manalokas was basking in the glow from above and Aliki, watching, realised that Elena could no more help assimilation of the person with whom she talked than others could stand back from the possibility of it. Elena's eyes shone with their developing cat-night vision, the silver eye shadow stretching expression outwards, the pupils of her eyes black and large.

As the captain stepped towards the door, his officers broke free of the group and Aliki, moving quickly and putting a restraining hand on the chief purser's sleeve, said, 'Please, have you a minute?'

Mr Kondomanolio considered his situation, looked towards his captain for affirmation and said, 'Ye...es?'

'Thanks.'

Others were leaving. 'Goodbye.'

'Lovely party. Goodbye.'

'Goodbye.'

'Delightful party.'

She regarded the chief purser carefully and said, 'I want to tell you that I've seen, I mean I *think* I've seen a man on the Sun Deck who, well, who doesn't really seem to be on the cruise. Can you help?'

Mr Kondomanolio's cold eye examined the passenger. He said, 'I suggest you go back to the deck where you *think* you saw him and have another look.'

'I have, several times.' She felt herself blush and tried not to see the disillusionment in the chief purser's eyes. 'But he is ne ... never there,' she stuttered. 'Or only in the dark so that I can't see him properly.' She offered Mr Kondomanolio another drink and when he declined and turned towards the door, she said, 'Don't go. If I describe the man to you, do you think you could consider your list?'

'Mrs Findlay, this is not a police unit. We do not attach description to name.'

'Please,' she hurried on, 'let me describe him. He is short, slight, youngish, has black curly hair, and ... and I think he may be Greek.'

'...There are twenty male Greek passengers on board, and although short could fit all, not one is either slight or young-ish.' The chief purser had his leg towards the door. 'Are you sure he is Greek?'

'Perhaps from Crete,' she said. 'Besides, he looks Greek.'

Mr Kondomanolio allowed himself a smile. What could this English lady know about it? 'And how is that?' he said finally.

'As I've said, short but powerful. And, well, giving out an aura of self-confidence.'

The chief purser wondered if the lady was trying to flat-ter information out of him. 'Yes,' he said, 'you have described the typical Greek. One of millions.'

'He has nearly perfect English,' she persisted, knowing she'd had only a few words with him, and knowing also that Mr Kondomanolio could not or would not help. 'If you could perhaps look at your list of Italians, say, or ...'

'I suggest that the next time you see this man, you send for me. Thank you for the party.'

He had gone and, shutting the door, she stood facing it. How ridiculous she had been.

Turning back into the cabin, she saw that Nikos was stand-ing there.

'Nikos! You've been listening.'

'Is good thing. Now I put you right.' He began to collect the glasses.

'What do you mean? Put me right?' She felt her voice rising.

Nikos stopped rubbing the dirty glasses with his clean dry cloth and looked directly at her. 'Is no good, this man. Is not there.'

'How dare you?' She had her mother's voice.

He stood in the middle of the cabin, his frame beginning to vibrate. 'Mrs Findlay,' it was the first time he had mastered the pronunciation, 'it is too much moon-looking.' He turned round and, without his usual swish and whirl, made for the door. 'So sorry,' he said as he went into the corridor.

She could feel tears of frustration forming. Why had Nikos said what he had? And why had the chief purser implied the same illusion? Carl Roberts had not mocked or laughed in her face. Or had he? And yet, Oh God! She was making a fool of herself. She was glad now she had not talked to Elena about it. Elena would have said why go out after someone who doesn't appear to exist when there are plenty who do?

She shut her eyes from the prospect of her own reflection in the glass, and behind her lids came the vision of a small man with smiling eyes and brush eyelashes partly covering them. He *did* exist. She sat with her legs up on the bed, her back to the wall, and switched off the bedside light. At first the movement was in herself, a trembling in her limbs, and then she saw the garden shimmer awake, this time herself walking in it. She touched the shrubs and flowers that were around her, and as the small man just ahead of her, wearing a tunic slit at the sides up to the waist, stretched out an arm as if to present the scene to her, she became part of it.

She snapped on the light. These people did not make a cult of the dead. Here in this room there lingered the potent, herb-scented essence of them, the whole throbbing life force of them. She looked towards the door. 'Yes, Carl Roberts, forward-looking.'

Rising now, she straightened her dress, brushed her hair, saw that her face had resumed its usual guarded expression and walked along the passageway to join her mother in the dining room.

Tomorrow in the palace of Knossos she might get some clue as to whether her companion of the nights and early mornings belonged in this age or that.

The long blue and white coaches that made their way through the modern suburbs of Heraklion carried within them passengers from the *Laconia*, who, in spite of themselves, had become something of a unit. The forward movement of the ship, the majestic monotony of the Aegean Sea and the luminous and healing quality of the light had helped to bring about a sensation redolent of the rocking cot.

In the coach that carried the English-speaking passengers, the guide was attempting to awaken them from their long trance with a stream of pleasant and lightweight chatter. She was the guide about whom the captain and Peter Miller had had a few more words. 'Damn good she is,' the Major had said at Aliki Findlay's party, and the captain had answered, 'But she was probably the least knowledgeable.' 'What d'you mean?' Peter Miller had been incensed by the captain's bland statement and the captain, possibly getting back at the Major for earlier wayward attitudes, said that, of the four guides, the German-speaking was the most thorough. 'Bloody Krauts,' Peter Miller had replied, and the captain, stepping back from the spray of spit that accompanied the words, said that, whatever the Major's view might be, the fact was that the Germans knew their history. As it happened, Peter Miller was being forced to change his tune a little because acquaintance with Professor Friebel had shown him another side to the German face. To the amazement of his wife and Molly Wainwright and the surprise of the friends he had gathered, he had abandoned the idea of his solitary visit to the centre of the island to re-enact his wartime landing there, in favour of a journey with 'the girls' to some ancient palace at a place called Knossos. He knew already that all he'd find were more bloody columns and hordes of people, but, as Daphne had pointed out to him, he might as well be on any old cruise if he was going to divide his time between Costas, the backgammon board and his favourite place on the Sun Deck. 'It's not that Molly and I mind going on our own,' Daphne had said, 'but I think just a teeny bit of culture would be good for you.' As he'd said to the young woman now sitting beside him, 'At my stage of life, culture would be worse than useless.' Aliki, who had gradually found a magnetism in the Major's constant outspokenness, had replied, 'I'd do what you want'. Now, as a result of what she saw as the Major's studiously polite way of coming last on to the bus – to show any wandering 'Krauts' how such situations should be handled – the Major was not with 'the girls' but sandwiched between the professor and herself. She could see the professor was taking up extra room in order to ease his leg, while she, as Peter Miller had told her, was taking up less than her fair share because, as he put it, 'You are only ever partly there'. Aliki had laughed, knowing full well the Major had not bothered with her on the voyage, but now because her mood was sanguine and because she had bothered to do something with her usually straight, boyish hair, he stood up, offered to change places with her, giving her a place with the professor, and sat on the aisle seat where he turned to talk to Mr Fosdick.

'Lovely morning,' he said, and Mr Fosdick looking at his watch and remembering the light luncheon he had just eaten on board, answered, 'Yes, wasn't it.'

Aliki watched with a twinge of doubt as the Major leaned across to Mr Fosdick and asked, 'Having a jolly cruise? Been here before?'

'No. I've never been abroad.' Mr Fosdick turned to Audrey Martin as if for confirmation of this astonishing statement and Aliki, watching her mother, saw the look of irritation and sensed a new protection. 'Mr Fosdick has been too busy building up his business to have time for travel,' her mother said.

The look of distaste on Peter Miller's face was no indication that he was going to drop the subject. 'So now you're after a bit of Greek culture?' he said.

'They say that the palace of Knossos is the archetype of the Minoan palaces, and as King Minos is believed to have lived in this one I'm interested in it.'

Smiling now, Aliki studied her mother's look of triumph and glanced at her neighbour's discomfort. Mr Fosdick, she was pleased to see, was sitting high in his seat, having dispersed the potential atmosphere of patronisation.

'It's your choice, old boy, not mine. If it weren't for Daphne and Molly trying to inject culture into me ...' He left the sentence unfinished because by then Mr Fosdick was looking out of the window at all the possibilities around them.

'Don't be put off by this,' the professor was saying as he pointed to the dust-covered modern buildings on either side of the road. 'It is no indication of what is coming.' But Aliki, looking out of the window, was not put off. She had already glimpsed an impression of Mount Ida and, searching her memory, said, 'The birthplace of Zeus.'

' The rebellious spirit of the Cretan has kept the island in a state of revolt for centuries.' Professor Friebel was still talking and Frau Friebel, from her seat in front, turned to say, 'I believe their guerrillas gave the German soldiers a tough time during the war.'

Oh dear, Aliki thought, the war story from the Major will almost certainly follow, but for the moment Peter Miller was subdued.

As the coach turned off the main road, leaving behind the suburbs of Heraklion, the professor pointed out the villa *Adriana*, reminding them all that it had been built for the great archaeologist Sir Arthur Evans, and then looking straight down the road again he said, 'Heinrich Schliemann was always maintaining that evidence of a great civilisation lay beneath the mound of Knossos.'

There was no reaction from the Major, not even a sigh of restlessness.

Aliki wondered if she dare question the professor about the Minoan civilisation. He seemed tuned in to the subject, after all ... 'Do you think it was the feminine emphasis on, say, fertility and fruitfulness that made war seem inglorious to the Minoan?'

'Aliki.' It was her mother's firm voice. 'The professor is on holiday.' But the professor, ignoring the interruption, said, 'War is unnecessary if you have mastery of the seas. And yes, the Cretans did do something to free the human spirit from enslavement to its gods, particularly gods of war. But you would be failing in your understanding if you did not see the Minoan civilisation as a blending of the female and male principles.'

Husband and wife exchanged smiles and the professor, comfortably into his subject, continued, 'I am believing that in Knossos you may sense something of the lightness of touch that was characteristic of the Minoan.' The professor got slowly to his feet as the coach came to a standstill.

Collecting handbags, jackets, cameras, the passengers filed

neatly out of the coach and Aliki, watching the second coach arrive, saw Carl Roberts and Elena come first off it.

As she had anticipated, the walk up to the palace was among a crowd of noisy, often garishly dressed tourists, but she found that by keeping her eyes fixed on the palace she could shake off today's atmosphere in favour of a time when numbers were few and dress elegant. Once into the area that represented the main court – where Minoans would have idled, strolled, transacted business, discussed matters of the moment – she felt a juxtaposition of time, a reassembling of groups and the dispersal of her own.

She saw, walking towards her, women decked with gold chains and armlets, heads dressed with gold leaves, flower-headed pins stuck through the hair, and some with stars, sequin-like, sewn into their long, bell-shaped skirts. They turned to talk to their men, who – wearing apron-like tunics, open at the sides up the waist – were also adorned with gold bracelets, armlets, anklets and wore their hair long down their backs. As the visitors from behind began to catch up with her, she tried to blend one period with the other and the vision that was in front of her was of a man standing there in tunic-like dress, looking at her and smiling. She stumbled and held on to a pillar, and, looking again, saw that the tunic had turned itself into a twentieth-century pair of trousers and shirt and the armlet a broad-braceleted watch. The man walked ahead of her down many steps, and, following, she came to the throne room and saw in the ancient chair the goddess-priestess, of benign beauty; straight-backed and regal. The priestess held out a hand to gazelle-eyed ladies who were accepting on her behalf gifts of flowers and herbs from the princes of the court. They seemed all sweet of face, neat-featured and honey-coloured. Aliki held out a hand, but the hand that held hers was Elena's, who had come now into the vaults and whose scent belonged with these people. Down frescoed corridors Elena led her, moving freely among the visitors, and to a garden where a pair of giant bull's horns framed the breast-shaped mount of Jikta. Looking up, Aliki saw that evening was beginning to settle on the mountain, setting fire to it; and the sight of it, the female earth through the male horns, gave meaning to the professor's reference to the blending of the female and male principles. She nodded and smiled, and, allowing one of the Greek's arms to rest loosely round her, walked with her to the coach.

The coach moved smoothly down the road, the passengers silent, thinking of a people, who, thousands of years before, had developed a standard of living that had included bathrooms, flushing water closets and minutely planned drainage systems.

Almost under her breath, Aliki said, 'I actually saw some of the Minoans walking about.'

'I thought something like that was going on,' Elena smiled reassuringly.

'I wonder if perhaps I'm a little mad?'

'N... no.' Aliki could see she was weighing the possibility, but at the same time making light of it. 'Some of us are more receptive to atmosphere.' She took hold of Aliki's hand.

'You are lucky, chérie, you are living two lives.'

Exactly.

Professor Friebel, who looked up from the book he was studying and from which he had been taking notes, put a finger in his place and said quietly, 'At Mycenae there will be no reconstruction.'

'You are disappointed?' Aliki asked.

'Once again,' he said, 'but there is always the reminder of how it was structurally.'

'My impression was much more than structurally.'

'You may already have had something of it in your head.'

She felt pleased with the professor and, lapsing into silence, watched the evening light turn the modern buildings of Heraklion into pink cubes.

It was later, when seated on her bunk, that she allowed herself to think about the man she had seen change identity in Knossos. Had others witnessed it?

She sat on in the dark and failed to hear the key turn on the outside of the door. The first gong for dinner was sounding when a knock came on it. She called out, 'Come in.'

The door handle turned but there was no entry. She tried the handle from the inside and, realising that it was either jammed or locked, called, 'Who is it?'

'It is Doctor Anagnosti,' a voice said, and Aliki, speaking loudly, said, 'I think my steward may have locked the door.'

'I will find him,' the doctor called out, and she was left staring at the door.

There was another knock on the door, the sound of a key turning and this time Doctor Anagnosti came into the cabin.

'I understand that you did not feel well during the visit to Knossos. Can I help?'

She looked at him without answering and then, studying the receptive expression on his face, said, 'All that happened was that I stumbled for a moment when I saw a man I know dressed as a Cretan from antiquity.' She waited for the doctor to take this in. He nodded, and she said, 'Either I am seeing ghosts – in which case lucky me – or the man in question from the twentieth century had gone to visit the palace dressed in some scant garment. Either way I'm fortunate because it means that the spirit of this person is strong enough to haunt both my daytime awareness and my dreams.' She folded her arms across her chest.

He said, 'Perhaps if you walk close to history you can see visions from the past.'

'No. History sometimes frightens me. It's as if we are powerless against it.' She leaned towards the small man who resembled some of those she had seen walking in the palace that day. 'There is someone on this ship who is haunting both my thoughts and vision of life. And now today he was in the palace.' She stood straight.

'I understand.'

'I would prefer that you did not patronise me.'

Doctor Anagnosti had spotted the whisky bottle in the open cupboard, and it reminded him that in the hospital he could be both physician and host. He said, 'Why do you not come back to the hospital where we can talk while I keep an eye on my patient?'

Aliki reached in to the cupboard. 'How is your patient?' She poured the whisky. 'Nikos has no right to shut me in. He takes on far too much responsibility for his passengers.'

'My patient is doing well, the girl is attentive now.' He looked carefully round the room and his eyes lingered at the fresco on the wall. 'Describe this man to me.'

'Actually, I'm not interested in describing him to you. I'm interested in knowing if you think there is some physical phenomenon here, something on the ship that has caused first Tessa to reverse the truth about herself, then change her mind and now my juxtaposition in time. Is there some ...' she hesitated, remembering the Greek source of the word she wanted, '*catalyst* on board?'

'Journeys release things from the psyche.'

Aliki smiled. She would have been disappointed if this kindly, practical-minded Greek had indulged her. She said, 'You don't believe I have seen this man.'

'It is what *you* believe that matters. If seeing him is freeing you somehow, then ...'

She held out her hand. 'I am glad you came. Shall I see you again?'

'No. No, it will not be necessary.'

The doctor turned to go and Aliki said, 'About your patient, is she going to be all right?'

'Yes. The catalyst is working on her too.' He grinned. 'By the time we return to Venice she may *walk* off the ship.'

After the doctor had departed Aliki pressed the bell marked 'steward': she would tell him off. But almost immediately Nikos and his black-toothed grin was in the doorway. 'You rang, Mrs Findlay?' Aliki said, 'Thank you for looking after me.'

The grin remained and through it Nikos said, 'No need now to go on deck.'

She suppressed anger. 'If I do go on deck I want you to know that I shall be all right.'

Nikos swept the yellow duster over the dressing-table and pirouetted out of the room. She heard him talking to himself and was glad that she did not know his language.

She took off her daytime dress and stepped into the freshly pressed cotton print. Selene tonight would merely be the torchbearer for what she wanted to see; she had already said goodbye to the seductive goddess.

Up on the top deck, she stood where the night breezes caressed her neck and shoulders. She heard the rush and slap of the ship's bow in the water. Light was from the phosphorescence that hovered over the water and from the thousand million miles away stars a thousand million years old.

She wondered if anyone else was on deck and saw a couple disappear behind a lifeboat, as, turning, she watched a figure come out of the shadows.

He said, 'I saw you in Knossos today.'

'Were you … I mean … are you … was it …?'

He put a hand towards hers on the rail and she moved hers nearer to his. 'Everyone on the ship denies knowledge of you.'

'Everyone?' His laugh vibrated into her. '*They* know I am here.'

'They?'

'The ship's crew.'

'You mean … you mean …?'

'A member of it.'

Defiant laughter choked her throat. Wouldn't Audrey be pleased.

'But your uniform … where is it?'

'That is why I come late night and early morning. We are not allowed on deck without a uniform.'

Now that he was out of the shadows she could picture him balancing elegant glasses on a tray, except that it was not a tray, nor was it glasses, it was a vessel being offered to the Queen, the Earth Goddess.

'You say you're from Crete?'

'Many on this ship.'

'And what is your work, you crew member with perfect English?'

'In the engine-room.'

'Without ambition?'

'The pleasures of the moment.' He moved closer. 'Each day I have found a place to watch you. Beauty should be shared between those who possess it and those who recognise it.' He laughed again and she suddenly felt beauty descend on her.

They began to walk round the deck – perfectly in step. A few passengers passing in the dark saw them so harmonised that they were as one.

She smelled the salt on his clothes, also oil, and, beneath, a herbal smell of the garden at Knossos. She said, 'Some say you are thought up out of my dreams.'

He stopped smiling and looked directly at her. 'You must decide.'

'Can we meet in full daylight?' She stretched her arm backwards as if to dismiss the night.

'Come with me when the ship docks in Venice. There could be days in the sun.'

'When the ship docks in Venice I must go home.'

'Must?'

'Well ...'

They were walking again round the deck and, as their pace quickened and the night became thicker and darker, she felt him move away.

'All right,' she called out. 'In Venice. But first you must come to me in my cabin. Tonight, later, when the ship is asleep.'

'It is never asleep.'

'I'm on A Deck, in cabin ...'

'... I know where you are.'

She held out a hand, but he had already gone, merging this time fully into the dark.

Alone now, she felt afraid. Did she want this … this crew member in her cabin? She walked towards the rails and held on to them. Was she prepared to believe that he was a member of the crew? She turned and went towards the gangway. Light in the ship's interior seemed very bright after the darkness outside, and voices were pitched to something like a party mode. Her legs, which had seemed so light and springy when she had begun the evening walk, were now like wood, and she felt the weight of her footsteps on the stairway. One, two, three, she began to count.

Should she perhaps reassure Audrey that, following her upset at Knossos, she was all right? Audrey had not been with her at the time but Nikos, who had told the doctor, might also have given the news to her mother. Audrey might come looking for her in the cabin, and what if she ran into the member of the crew? Aliki sucked in her breath but dismissed the idea. Her mother was too taken up with Mr Fosdick to give thought to her daughter.

Going down the stairway, she looked into the lounges, the bars and finally the games room.

Seated at the roulette table were Audrey, Mr Fosdick, Peter Miller and Daphne Miller. Molly Wainwright sat beside her friend, a long drink in one hand and a cigarette in the other. At the big table, Carl Roberts and Elena were playing baccarat. It was a night for full evening dress; the long dresses and black ties gave to the room an atmosphere of reserve and elegance that helped to counter some of the avaricious looks cast about at the tables.

If she interrupted now she would draw attention to herself, and almost certainly Audrey would interpret the expression on her face as something to be examined. She searched her bag and wrote a note to her mother telling her she was all right but was tired and was going to bed. Oh God! Why had she asked him to come? She folded the piece of paper carefully and slowly tiptoed further in to the room. Bending, she whispered in Molly Wainwright's ear, 'I don't want to disturb the game, but please give this to my mother when it's finished.'

Molly Wainwright looked up and, from the twinkle in her eye, Aliki guessed that this particular woman might have caught on to something of her secret life. Smiling she whispered, 'All right.'

Aliki went down the last flight to A Deck, sought reassurance from exchanging goodnight wishes to one or two passengers and went to her cabin.

Nikos was sitting on the stool in the passageway two cabins beyond Aliki's, and when he saw the lady come towards him, wearing the prettiest of her two dresses and with a flush on her face, he thought of the last conversation he'd had with her. He unlocked her cabin door and, deciding to make a joke of his fears, said, 'Was it good on deck tonight? Is good you tell me if there is something you want.'

'Oh no! Thanks. I was just wondering what time you manage to finish work.'

'Work never finish, but I go now. Goodnight, Mrs Findlay.' Nikos hesitated, then slowly walked down the passageway.

'Goodnight Nikos,' she called after him.

Now she was alone, and the fresco above the dressing-table that normally came to life at her bidding remained obstinately still She tried to recapture her new relationship with the sunlight by taking off her dress and examining her skin. She took a bottle of body lotion from the dressing-table drawer and, unscrewing the top, smelled the mixture of eucalyptus and honey. Alternating strokes with pats, she smoothed the lotion into her skin and wondered what she would do with the next couple of hours as the ship's passengers played. If ever she needed her own type of music it was now. Perhaps a mixture: some Bob Dylan or the Prokofiev violin concerto. She turned on the ship's radio hopefully, but a news bulletin was being read in Greek. She switched the knob and, finding some Greek music, followed the rhythm, dancing round the cabin. Round and round. She stopped in front of the mirror and spoke to her reflection. What would it be like to dance with … What was his name? How strange that they spoke, watched each other, had even the feeling of being together, and yet, didn't know what the other was called. Did he know her name? Oh God! Did he know the number of her cabin? Had she given it to him just before he left her on the deck? If he didn't know her name, and didn't know her cabin number, then … Yes, she was sure she had given him the number. She would call him Alexis. At first he had been like a dream remembered, then a shadow of that dream, thereafter a figure that fitted into the fantasy, and then a manifestation of what she believed to be the beautiful people of long ago, and ... Oh God! Now she had been told that he was a present-day member of the crew. She laughed. She would see him as a Minoan seaman of long ago. Would he come?

Would it be a good idea to undress completely or stay as she was? Perhaps she could telephone the next cabin and find out if Tessa would like to come in for a chat. She looked at her wristwatch: it was past midnight and Tessa, probably exhausted from her hours in the hospital, would be asleep. She sat on the bench with her towel round her shoulders and looked in at the cabin: the interior had taken on a glow that, she hoped, was coming from the centre of her mind. Whether or not Alexis came to her now was not of primary importance. Then what was? Her present state of mind. She turned to look out through the porthole at the opaque sky that was like a canvas prepared for ... for what? For the picture she would paint of the void that had been in her interior. She laughed scornfully: how could a void be depicted? She would, *could*, fill the void. If she didn't fill the void, might not the family ... family illness creep in? Had it already taken hold? She breathed in deeply. No. Who was it who had said that the origin of madness was the violent casting out of the mind that which *really* existed in favour of that which did not. Oh God! But Alexis did exist.

She began to walk again round the room. Round and round. When was the last reality? Long ago in Ireland, when her father had come out in the morning, wearing breeches and brandishing a crop, she had run ahead of him into the stables to be the first to smell the horse flesh in the early morning. She had run her nose and mouth all over her father's favourite mare and the sweet steam of its breath had merged with her own. For a gallop or two she was in front of her father on the horse, and the caress of the wind, the feel of his body behind had, yes, had been the reality.

She stopped in her movement round the room, shut her eyes. She could feel the warmth of heaving flesh beneath her thighs, the rolling movement of the horse's gait, the secure grasp of her father's arm.

Oh God! Could she hold on to the memory?

She moved towards the shower. If she let her thoughts dwell too long on the subject of her father and his death, she might sink back into the period following it. The pain had been alleviated by life at boarding school, followed by the visit to the old crone and her injunction: "Tis ruled by Fate ye're'. She had seen it as the easy, and only, way out, had climbed on the back of fate as she might have her father's mare and had been guided from behind. Well now, because of what she had found amongst her grandfather's books, she had been back to see the old woman, and almost joyfully was accepting that she 'would be going on a journey', the happy platitude an indication that the void would be left behind. "Tis ruled by Fate' had come to have less meaning since she had been looking at it in defiance.

Running the water all over her body, she thought of Elena. What would Elena do in the present situation? Elena would not be in this situation because her contacts would have been made before starting on the cruise; everything else would be a bonus she could handle.

Elena would take a shower and, like the women of ancient Greece, would oil herself all over and climb on to the bed.

There was a knock on the door and, pulling the bathroom door shut, she called out, 'Who is it?'

It would be Nikos checking to see if she were all right. Why couldn't he leave things now to the night steward?

Tessa's voice said, 'I was wondering if you were okay?'

Wrapping the towel round herself, Aliki came out into the cabin, opened the door and gave Tessa a hug. Tessa looked pleased. 'I heard you talking to yourself,' she said, 'and wondered if perhaps you were lonely.'

Was this an excuse to come into her cabin?

Aliki looked at the small face, large bright eyes, tawny hair and saw Tessa as a woodland nymph who had wandered from the dark into the light and was wondering whether to stay. 'It's nice to see you, but shouldn't you be asleep?'

'Since my mother's illness time has become a bit unreal. Sometimes I'm with her at night, sleeping during the day.'

'I missed you on the coach going to Knossos. Were you with your mother last night?'

'Yes.'

'Does the doctor visit her at night?'

'I think the doctor must set his alarm because he appears at least twice every night. I have a feeling my mother waits for him before finally going to sleep.'

'Which he knows, I suppose.'

Tessa walked over to the open wardrobe and fingered the evening dress. 'You don't join in the dancing after dinner. Don't you like it?'

Should she tell Tessa about her encounter on the deck this evening, on other evenings and the rendezvous that was about to take place? She looked again at her watch, and Tessa, following the gesture, said, 'I guess you want to sleep.'

'No. It's just that ...'

'Is someone coming?' Tessa's eyes seemed suddenly all pupil.

'Oh no. I mean, yes.' She'd said it and felt better that the knowledge was shared. She shut the door on the bottle of whisky.

'In a little while,' she said.

Tessa looked at Aliki wrapped in the bath-towel, at the open bottle of lotion on the dressing-table, at the preparation generally and in a small voice, almost a whisper, asked, 'Who is he?'

'As a matter of fact, I don't really know.' Aliki laughed, both to cover her embarrassment and to include Tessa in the complicity.

'But...'

'I mean I don't know *exactly* who he is. I know that we've been together once or twice and feel we have known each other for a long time.'

'I'll leave you now,' Tessa said. 'To prepare.' Her eyes were on the second bottle. The bottle of oil. She looked round the cabin once more, and, watching her expression, Aliki said,

'If you like, I'll lock the door, then we can just talk.'

'No!' Tessa held out both hands towards her. 'I'm going back to the hospital.'

Aliki held on to Tessa for a moment. 'Thank you for coming. Please give my love to your mother.'

She shut the door behind Tessa, turned the key. This time she must finish her preparations. She brushed her hair and hesitated, looking towards the cupboard. She must be ready for when he comes. She poured. Put the top on the bottle. Just one drink followed by a glass of water would be all right. At this hour of night it was reasonable to smell slightly of drink.

She sat in the armchair facing the door and the whole encounter with him on deck was played back to her as on a movie screen. She did not want the retrospection of it. She wanted the real-life encounter, here, now. Was she already putting it safely into a pocket of memory? Oh God! Why didn't he come? She looked at her watch. It wouldn't be safe yet. He would run into passengers. Fear took another tug at her stomach, and the panic of a failed meeting with him became more real than the prospect of an encounter. The whisky in the glass was gone and she poured another. After all, the smell of two drinks would have about the same potency as the smell of one. If her father hadn't left her at the start of her adolescence she would not now be behaving as if she were just into it. Oh God! If only her life with Audrey hadn't been a series of minor dramatics, she would know now how to cope in a real-life situation. But was it a real-life situation? Clandestine meeting in the dark with someone who might even be a shadow did not constitute reality. But he was someone. He was a member of the crew. She laughed. It would be fun to tell her mother. But Audrey couldn't protest. What about little Mr Fosdick? Yes, what about him? She would think through the relationship between her mother and Mr Fosdick later, and tomorrow she would talk to Audrey about it. After Alexis had been.

She must keep moving in case she should fall asleep. With the glass in her hand she walked backwards and forwards and thought of the progress of Audrey and Mr Fosdick round the deck. Was her mother remoulding the man? Adjusting him to her own tastes? Or was Mr Fosdick, with his neat, precise ways and his neat, admiring manner, the antithesis of the wide, yes, loud, all-life-embracing figure of her father? Was Mr Fosdick somebody in his own right? She had never really known what the relationship was between Audrey and her father, only that she was jealous of it.

She sank once more into the chair and the damp warmth of the towel acting against the temperate warmth of the air-conditioned room brought her close to sleep. Her head nodded and, just at the point where she was about to enter into a dialogue with Alexis, sleep absorbed her.

Towards morning, when a metal-grey light crept into the cabin, she woke to the realisation that she was facing a locked door.

~❀~

The grey light that had crept into Aliki's cabin was lifting now from the whole of the ship and disappearing starboard in a shimmering haze. The captain, who had been on the bridge early, contemplating the thick mist around them, smiled now at the light that was balancing in golden saucers on top of the waves. The ship would drop anchor around midday at Nauplio for Mycenae, an excursion, the captain thought to himself, from which the passengers always returned contemplative. The separate units throughout the ship seemed bound now into one large group and, in talking to the excursion officer on this morning of the long journey inland, the captain was further encouraged to learn that there had been a blending of nationalities in the various coaches. It wasn't necessary for his officer to explain whom he meant when he said that there was still one Englishman reluctant to mix.

'I do not know why that sort of man travels,' the excursion officer said to his captain, and Captain Manoli, speaking to him in English, said, 'At a certain time of the year one gets out of England, don't you know.' The finer nuance of expression was lost on the younger man, who had limited English.

'What I do not understand about the Englishman,' the excursion officer continued, 'is his insistence on making these trips. Within minutes of departure in the coach he is asking if we are nearly there.' Captain Manoli knew that the old adage 'It is better to travel than to arrive' did not apply to the children of the world, and, of the children he had known,

Major Miller was turning out to be, surprisingly, about the most endearing. There was a certain charm about his inflexibility of attitude, because, as the captain knew, the other side of that coin would be the Major's extreme reliability in time of crisis. Crisis had not come their way and now, with a bright sun and blue sky to signal departure, the passengers were once again gathered beside the exit on A Deck.

'Good morning, Captain. It is today that we look on the face of Agamemnon.'

Captain Manoli smiled. Many a classical scholar had passed this way, had gone to the home of Greek antiquity and had examined in detail the palace–fortress of the war-like race. Discussion at dinner the same evening was always about the Greeks in relation to Homer's Achaeans, and these in relation to the actual burial place of the king, Agamemnon. The Germans insisted, because their hero Professor Schliemann had told them so, that one of the two beehive tombs found there was that of Agamemnon, while others argued that it was actually the tomb of an earlier king. Captain Manoli knew that Agamemnon was not buried there, but he kept the controversy alive as it was in the interest of further tours for him to do so, in the same way that he allowed visitors such as Aliki Findlay to believe that in her chosen period of antiquity – the Minoan – emphasis had been on love and fertility. It was proving difficult to keep from keen enthusiasts the recent belief that in another palace in Crete human sacrifice had been made. For his part, he preferred to see his people as having liberated man from the domination of the gods, and to have lifted women – God bless them all – to an equal, if not superior position. He looked round the crowded exit, saw the tall blonde figure of Elena bending slightly to listen to the lively chat from the English Mrs Miller and thanked the gods – he meant God – for her constant return to their ship. She was a sight and an influence that kept passengers and crew happy, and he had stopped long ago wondering about her age because she didn't seem to have one. He bowed in response to her greeting and, turning once more to Professor and Frau Friebel, wished them Godspeed from the land where the gods were known to interfere in the lives of humans.

up the inner companionway, the captain stopped briefly in front of the wall mirror. He pulled out creases in his uniform jacket, stepped backwards to get a more objective view and accidentally walked on to the outstretched foot of Aliki Findlay on her way up. Aliki accepted his apology and wondered if she could ask him the question that she had been trying out since she woke this morning.

She said, 'Can all members of the crew get into cabins at any time?'

Captain Manoli moved Mrs Findlay slightly to the right, nodded to passengers going up and down and, with a hand on the knot of his tie, said, 'Is something missing from your cabin?'

'Oh no! It's just that ...'

'Yes?'

'I wondered if there is a master key.'

'Mrs Findlay, you can rest assured that only you and your most trusted steward can get into your cabin.'

'That is what I was afraid of.'

'Please?'

'It's all right.' She smiled warmly at the man who was so much the support and prop to all their concerns and wishes, and decided for the sake of any future prospect of seeing Alexis not to alert the captain's suspicions. Instead she told him that, no, she wasn't going to visit Mycenae, and, yes, she was going to the Sun Deck, perhaps to chat to some of the ship's officers and crew.

Captain Manoli stiffened. 'I think it is best that the men be not disturbed while they are on duty.'

'And how about off duty?' she dared, her eyes sparkling, and the captain, remembering something that had been dropped to him by the chief purser, said, 'You know, Mrs Findlay, if there is some problem disturbing you I wish you would come to me.'

'Thanks. When there is, I will.' She slung her bag over her shoulder, turned on her heel and went up the stairway.

The captain returned to the bridge, entered his day cabin and sat at the large flat desk on which maps and charts were laid out under a glass top. He rang down for the chief purser.

'Well, Chief,' he said to his compatriot, who was very soon saluting in front of him, 'I think you are right. We shall have to make some enquiries amongst members of the crew. It looks as if the rumour about Mrs Findlay is true. Have you given any further thought to which of the men it might be?'

'It should not be too difficult to locate him, sir, providing we can accept that the passenger is *actually* seeing this person.'

'I heard that at Knossos our passenger had a slight dizzy spell as a result of seeing, well, of seeing a ghost. It seems that the lady witnessed the transference of a twentieth-century male into some phantom of what she called the Minoan period.'

'I see.'

'Of course it was all in her imagination. For this reason I am inclined to dismiss her claim that she has been talking to some man on this ship, who, she says, never appears except during the hours of darkness.'

'Who told you of the incident?' The chief purser's eyes narrowed.

'The doctor.'

'The doctor does not imagine things.'

'Doctor Anagnosti thinks that Mrs Findlay is capable of believing what she thinks she sees. In other words, if she wants to.'

In step the two men turned starboard. 'Keep an eye on it, Chief.' The captain dismissed his officer and, moving on to the bridge wing to speak to the officer of the watch, considered activity on the deck below. Deck stewards were busy with buckets and brushes, and from his position on the bridge the captain watched the silent movement and wondered if he should develop a more perceptive view of some of his men.

Close to the stewards, but hidden in the shadow of one of

the lifeboats, Aliki also watched activity. Her eyes flitted from one face to another, her mind calling up details of Alexis. This one? No. That? She could see he was not there.

Running now down the companionway, she went into the Verandah Deck lounge and on to the stool in front of Costas.

Costas knew. His cousin Nikos kept him in touch with gossip both above and below deck. That the pale English lady had a secret rendezvous on deck in the moonlight with what she believed to be a member of the crew distressed his correct-minded cousin but caused him a great deal of thinly disguised pleasure. It was just the sort of thing to make those white-uniformed officers get off their complacent backsides. That the moonlight meetings were all in the mind of the lady in question was something he chose not to consider.

Now he smiled innocently at her, seated squarely on the stool. He reached for the cocktail shaker to begin her whisky sour and surreptitiously turned his wristwatch the wrong side up in case she should see the time and decide against a drink.

'Thank you, Costas,' she said sipping and licking the sugar off her top lip, 'you make it like no one else in the world.'

Costas was used to flattery, abuse, confession, admonition, rejection, even ridicule, and he had more or less the same slightly condescending smile to greet them all. This morning, because he hoped to have an interesting and revealing conversation with the lady, he gave Mrs Findlay the kind of warm look that he reserved for those he met only on shore.

Aliki lifted the glass to her lips once more, looked over

the rim at the active man behind the bar and, fixing him with her eyes, said, 'Is there a Greek on board who speaks nearly perfect English? Of the ship's company, I mean.'

Costas thought. The easy answer to that was, of course, the captain. But he would not insult the lady by playing with what seemed to be a serious discussion.

'The officers all speak some English.'

'I meant crew, Costas.'

Costas wiped the bar with a wet cloth, emptied the used ashtray, ran the tap over it, dried it, returned it to the bar and stood silently observing his customer. He was actually non-plussed. Such openness amazed him. The sensation was so rare that for a moment he ran it around his head, savouring it.

'Stavros Zervudachi from the engine-rooms has good English, he has an English mother.'

'And is he good-looking and small?' Aliki was enjoying herself, and watched with amusement the expression on the face of the barman, who clearly had never considered the looks of this engine-room crew member.

'Yes. He is small. Why you ask about this man?'

'Because there is a Greek with good English whom I talk to sometimes on deck, but he is not a passenger.'

'Which deck do you talk?'

'Does it matter?' She laughed and the sound of it disturbed some solitary drinkers in the lounge. They looked up through clouded eyes, then focused once more on the glass in front of them.

Costas leaned a little forward, complicity now giving resonance to his voice. 'I take a note to this man?'

'No, thank you.' She needed more time to think. Could she trust Costas? It seemed probable that Alexis was this Stavros Zervudachi working in the engine-rooms. Silently she stared into her glass. The more she thought about it the more she realised how difficult it must have been for him the other night. She forgave him for not rattling at the door or making a noise when he found the cabin door locked. The point, she realised, was that there had been a locked door between her and Alexis, and she had locked it. She stared at Costas, wondering if she dared risk a note.

'Yes, please, Costas,' she said in answer to the raised arm with the cocktail-shaker. She drank in silence as her eyes travelled from one side of the bar to another, Costas watching her movement.

She sat and sipped and stared in front of her. If Alexis had come to find a locked door, what would have been his reaction? That she had changed her mind? That she had forgotten? Fallen asleep? What could he have done about it? Nothing. What was there to be done about it? He could wait and see. She could wait and see. No. That is what she was not going to do. She was not going to provide fate with another convenient void.

'Thanks, Costas,' she said, and ran quickly from the room, almost jumped her way down two flights of stairs, calling out 'sorry' to one or two passengers with whom she collided and, reaching the exit on A Deck, managed to squeeze in between some of the passengers in the last departing tender.

The coach ride was long and the German-speaking guide in the coach for Italians was having difficulty explaining in English – because she spoke neither Italian nor Greek – the muddle over departure. There had been the usual rush for the tenders, but because one of the tenders had broken down halfway between ship and the shore, the last batch of passengers had been herded all into one. Now, amused by the atmosphere that had developed inside the coach, Aliki thought of the captain and his determination to keep his mixed family in a state of grace. The Australian woman with a large, often-exposed bosom, bright red hair and loud voice, who had attempted from time to time to join with the little unit formed by Peter Miller, was protesting that the even larger German woman next to her was overlapping into her seat. Abuse in a mixture of languages took on the quinine-like flavour of inter-family strife, the German lady getting to her feet and shouting, 'But what can you expect from someone of a former colony?' and ceasing only when the coach took a sudden swerve. Laughter and apology took the place of anger and vituperation.

Carrying the laughter with her as she moved on to the mountain that led to Mycenae, Aliki slowed her pace to equal that of the professor and his wife. Slipping her arm inside his as they walked through the massive Lion Gate where no reconstructors had been at work, she listened to the professor as he suggested that the grip of the ancient people still held fast. They stopped, looked round, sniffed the air and were subdued by the aura that clung to the remains of a once-great city–state.

Hesitating in her walk for a moment, in case the spirits of their gods might mock this twentieth-century cavalcade, Aliki looked down vertical walls, along straight corridors, through underground passages, and wondered if her own enslavement to a paternity was being diminished by the catholic views of a German professor.

'I am equal with you, Gods,' she called out, turning to include the professor and his wife. He, now leaning on both his stick and his wife, spoke loudly, 'My word, how mortals take the gods to task.'

Laughter from them all echoed through the ruins and round the mountain...

On the way down the mountain Aliki gave only half an ear to the professor's discourse on the war heroes of long ago; instead, she thought of the other force that works in mankind: the force that keeps people at home, contemplating, asking questions, trying to find answers, accepting situations that are actually there. For herself, she would cease her moon-gazing, have no more truck with the seductive goddess. She would let the sun rays warm her, she would see the sun's reflection in the pools of water at her feet and when there were doubts she would take off her shoes and let the soil creep up between her toes.

~✲~

Later that night, when the second sitting for dinner was spread throughout the dining room, Aliki sat at the captain's table and learned from conversation around her that others beside Professor Friebel and his wife had opinions – as well as the facts – about Greek antiquity. She admired the captain's skill in appearing to answer and yet leave as a mystery some questions these scholars put to him. How many, she wondered, really wanted the definitive answer to their life's interest? For her part, she was prepared now to accept that there *might* be a flaw in what she had seen as the perfect Minoan civilisation – in the same way as she was prepared to accept that some on the ship might say there was not an Alexis.

She tried it out on the captain, as she had on Costas, and, not waiting for any preliminaries, said, 'Are there certain crew members who wander about the ship sometimes in civilian dress?'

'Mrs Findlay, I am sorry that the passengers on this voyage have been of such little interest to you that your thoughts have turned to the ship's company. The company are here to serve and not to obtrude personally.'

She ignored the rebuke but felt the captain might know. 'No one has obtruded. It's just that from time to time I have seen on this ship, at night and early morning, a man whom I never see during the day.'

'And you would like to meet him more often?' The captain beamed. He had decided that the best way of laying this particular ghost was to confront her with it. There had been phantoms and fantasies before.

'Tomorrow is Sunday,' he said, 'and although we do not normally hold religious services on account of all the denominations, it would be possible if you wish.'

'But it is our last day!'

'And I can order the entire ship's company and all of the passengers to be on deck for morning service, in English, just for you.'

'Those in the engine-rooms would not be able to attend, would they?' The captain examined the look of innocence in her eyes and knew that he had made his point.

'You are right. For the purpose of keeping the ship afloat some cannot attend.'

'In that case,' Aliki said smiling, 'we could not achieve our aim.'

'Nor could we,' the captain concurred.

Discussion at the table became general again, and it was only later in the night, in conversation with the chief purser, that the captain said, 'As far as Mrs Findlay is concerned – as the English say – I think we have narrowed the field.'

'Surely, sir, you are not still believing in this man?' The chief purser was adamant.

'No. But if *she* believes, at least we've narrowed him down to the engine-rooms. Goodnight, Chief.'

'Goodnight, sir.'

On the last day of the cruise, as the ship sailed out of the Ionian into the Adriatic Sea, passengers turned their eyes inwards to reassess fellow guests and give final attention to their suntan.

Midships on the Sun Deck, Mr Fosdick was to be seen putting two deck chairs close to the rails as if to be out of earshot of some of the other passengers. There was a determined look to the neat features of the small Englishman, and the prominent moustache, brushed and groomed, had a jaunty air about it, so that Aliki, coming across the deck towards him, wondered what was in his mind. She shook his outstretched hand, and he, showing her into one of the deck chairs as if he had become host at his own party, sat also, leaning forward and offering a bag of peppermints.

'Thanks,' she said, swivelling in her chair and putting her hand into the striped bag. 'Have you been enjoying the cruise?' It was the first time she had addressed him properly and, now, smiling and watching him, she saw that in some pleasing way the long upper lip, munching on the sweet, reminded her of her father's favourite horse.

'The cruise has been the opening of a new life for me,' was Mr Fosdick's reply, and Aliki, popping the sweet in her mouth and sitting back in her chair, let the meaning reach her.

She sat still, munching and thinking and looking along the deck. She shot forward. Wasn't that Alexis on the companionway? She ran to the top of the stairs, but he had gone. And, looking down the shining metallic steps, she saw only recumbent figures, some in, some out of the sun. Sitting alert in the chair again she wondered, should she risk writing a note to this, this ... Stavros of the engine-rooms? She had been almost certain there would be one for her, slipped somehow into her cabin, telling her that Alexis had found a locked cabin the other night and, perhaps, fixing another rendezvous.

'Good morning, Aliki.' Her mother had come on deck and was settling now into the chair beside Mr Fosdick.

'Hello, Audrey.' Aliki pinned her hair on top of her head and, taking a few steps, dived into the pool. She swam strongly from end to end, floated on her back for a minute and, climbing out, reached for her towel.

She threw the towel over her shoulders, waved towards Mr Fosdick and Audrey and, crossing the deck, went down the companionway. Inside the Verandah Deck lounge she was met by a young duty officer who said, 'You cannot come in here dressed as you are,' and she, looking down at the towel wrapped now round her middle, said, 'Sorry, I wasn't thinking.' Rapidly she went down two more flights, through a quick change in her cabin, back again and finally on to the stool in front of Costas.

'All right, you can take the man a note from me.'

'Good morning, Mrs Findlay.' He had been practising her name. 'It is a good morning.'

'Very nice.' She had written a hurried note in her cabin, and now, bringing it out of her bag, asked, 'What was the name of the crew member with the good English?'

'Stavros Zervudachi.' She wrote the name on the envelope, knowing that she preferred the name Alexis, and held out her hand against the whisky sour now in the shaker.

The disappointment on Costas's face was lost on Aliki, who had spotted Peter Miller come in through the glass doors and make for the bar. His face was a blotchy, sunburnt red and he had the look of one who had been up all night.

'Bloody women! Would you believe it!' He sat on the bar stool beside her and, looking at Costas, said, 'Brandy, please.' Sliding the note under the ashtray, Aliki drew Costas's attention to it and climbed down from the stool.

'Don't go, *please*.' Peter Miller held out a restraining hand.

'What's wrong?'

'They're going to leave me.'

'Who?'

'The women.'

'For good?' She suppressed a smile.

'They say so. Bloody women.' Peter Miller took a large gulp of brandy and, turning to look at Aliki, said, 'I don't suppose I'll ever really understand it. Or them. I never wanted that woman Molly Wainwright in our lives, but Daphne insisted.'

'What's happened?' Aliki climbed back on to the stool.

'It's this ship. Daphne says something about seeing things clearly for the first time. Perhaps its the retsina or the sun.'

'Or perhaps the clarity of the light.'

'I knew I should never have encouraged this trip.'

'But, Major Miller, you were here during the war.'

'Don't call me Major Miller. It makes me feel a hundred.'

'Well, er, Peter, you had such an outstanding war, think of that.'

He sat upright. 'Daphne says I've made a fool of myself on the excursions. Never showing any real interest in the sights and always wanting to get back to the bar.' He drank again, the best five-star brandy going down his throat as if it were lemonade. She looked fully into his face and for the first time saw that in amongst the wrinkles and folds the eyes were a gentian blue. Once upon a time, before drink took over, he must have been a handsome man. 'She's going to leave me the house in Sussex, and she and Molly will be taking a flat together in London.' His face creased as if he might cry but instead he said, 'You see, they're not even leaving me my pride.'

'Oh, I don't think that's true.'

'She should keep the house and let me go away. It would look better that way.'

Aliki wondered how this man, so acutely conscious of himself, was able now to talk to her. Had he perhaps sensed that she also was making a fool of herself? She looked into the mirror behind the bar and saw from the reflection that her hand was resting over his.

'You'll find someone else.'

'What! At my age?'

'Age doesn't matter with men. It's …' She was going to say that it's experience that counts, but changed it to, 'It's being able to provide something. You will have your house, presumably money.'

'But at the end of it all there is only myself to offer.'

This time she put an arm round his shoulders. 'Don't forget,' she said, 'you've managed to absorb the attention of the most attractive woman on the ship.'

They both looked out through the window at the prone figure of Elena, parallel to the pool.

'If you can attract her,' Aliki continued, 'even for a short time, you may easily attract others...' She saw doubt in his eyes and added, with an affectionate grin, 'if not quite so beautiful.'

He smiled in return, but drank in silence, studying his own image in the mirror, and Aliki, who had now accepted the mixed cocktail from Costas, sat on, smiling reassuringly into the mirror, studying the man, who, perhaps for the first time, was facing some truth about himself.

After a time she said, 'Why don't we get the backgammon board. You could teach me the game.'

'Oh! Yes.' Peter Miller hurried from the lounge and Aliki, finding an empty table in the corner, turned to the barman. 'Please, Costas, not a word about my note, especially not to Nikos. When can you deliver it?'

'Tonight, when I go off duty.' Costas grinned, already a part of the plot.

Aliki and Peter Miller played an initial instructive game and then another, and as passengers came and went and the day became hotter and food less of an imperative, they stayed where they were, drinking longer drinks, their eyes glued to the board, their minds attempting to shut out personal problems. Aliki was almost certain that this evening her mother was going to tell her about Mr Fosdick and herself. She nodded now and again towards Audrey, who had brought in light snacks from the lunch table and who hovered over the dedicated instruction as if she herself might learn something from it. Towards evening, when she found she could both play backgammon and think of other things, Aliki allowed her thoughts to form the picture of Costas finding Alexis. Would Alexis look surprised? Pleased? Annoyed? Or would he accept the note with his usual air of calm? Would …?

'Don't forget you're coming to my cabin for drinks before dinner.'

Audrey was passing their table and Aliki, looking up, said, 'See you later.'

They played on, had more drinks and when Elena came to take her place, Aliki rose gratefully to her feet. The Major's smile was almost one of triumph and he thanked Aliki for the time she had spent with him.

On her way to her cabin Aliki thought about the subject she would let free this evening.

The sun had set by the time Aliki was seated in her mother's cabin. She was at an angle to the square room, trying not to see the bottle of champagne in an ice bucket in the bathroom basin.

'We've been lucky with our fellow passengers on this cruise,' Audrey began.

'Yes, they've been all right for a cruise but I don't want to see any of them afterwards.' She was not going to make it easy for her mother.

Audrey polished one of the three glasses brought in by Maria and said, 'Actually, darling, I wanted to tell you ...' She hesitated, put down the glass, picked up another.

'You want to tell me?' Aliki was watching her.

'How much better you are looking. Has something happened to you?'

'I was all right before I came on board.'

'No, you were not. You most certainly were not.'

Audrey stood close to her now, looking down at her, and Aliki, standing also, was an inch shorter.

'If you want to know,' Audrey continued, 'you've been pretty bloody awful for some years now.'

Slowly Aliki turned round to look fully into her mother's face. 'Why didn't you tell me that my grandfather is still alive?'

'I ... uh ... what are you talking about?'

'Don't bother to lie to me. I found the bills.'

'You mean to say you went through my private papers? How dare you!' Audrey's face had turned from white to pink. 'How dare you go through my desk?'

'It's no good, Audrey, the red herring won't work on this occasion. I want to know, and you are going to tell me why you lied to me all these years. Lied to everyone, that is.'

'I'm not going to justify myself to you,' Audrey protested.

'I was young when my grandfather became ill. If I'd been told the truth then I would have become used to the idea. How many more lies are there, Audrey?'

'There are no more lies.'

'So you admit there's been one? I'll tell you where there has been a lie – in the whole mode of our life. The ever-so-pleasant, day-to-day politeness of it. The clean, shining white brightness of it. Where were your feelings? Where were mine?' She whirled round as her mother moved away and, standing in front of her, said, 'You know what's the matter with you? You've outgrown the role of big sister.'

'I don't see what that has to do with your grandfather.'

'It has everything to do with our life.'

'I'd never have been into the role of big sister if you hadn't pushed me there.'

'*Me* push *you*!'

'Yes. If you couldn't have a father you wouldn't have a mother either. I've never been allowed to be a proper mother, caring for you, buying you pretty things, and ...'

'Is that what caring means – buying pretty things?'

'It was unnatural of you always wanting to climb into trousers, mucking about in the stables with the horses.'

Relief flooded through Aliki: so it had not been a false memory.

'Did you ever stop to think what it was like for me losing both my husband and, you might say, my daughter?'

'I think you're contemptible, trying for pity at this moment.' Her voice was calmer now, icier. 'Why did you never tell me about my grandfather's real illness? And his commitment?'

Audrey shuddered.

'Commitment,' Aliki said again.

Audrey turned round slowly and, holding on to the chair, sat down carefully. She pointed to the chair opposite and, obediently, Aliki sat. After a minute's silence, Audrey said, 'Until you've actually had to ... to commit someone you love to a psychiatric institution ...' she shut her eyes for a moment, opened them again to stare at Aliki, '... you can't know the effect it will have on you for the rest of your life.' Aliki watched her cross one leg carefully over the other. 'Your grandmother, you see, was unable, finally, to handle the situation, so I had to sign all the papers and go with your grandfather to the hospital.' She breathed deeply. 'After he had been taken in, when the door shut behind him, I had to drive home alone.' She nodded at the memory. 'When I returned to the house I went down to the little stream at the bottom of the garden and was sick as if the whole of my inside was coming up.' She gave a dry cough. 'I swore then I would never let anything happen to make me sick like that again, and I never have.' Her arms flopped from the chair arms on to her knee and Aliki, looking now carefully at her mother, saw the loose skin just forming under her chin.

Oh God! Perhaps Mr Fosdick really would care for her. He didn't see her as a failed mother, failed substitute for a father. He didn't see a woman who had to hold herself together with hairspray and face masks, someone who had to give nightly parties in case in solitude she would have the reminder of her father's illness and have to face what might be in herself. She hoped, yes, she really hoped, it wasn't just the looks that Audrey worked so hard to maintain that attracted Mr Fosdick. She hoped that he had some sort of vision of feminine need.

The telephone rang and, as Audrey stretched an arm to lift the receiver, Aliki guessed it would be Mr Fosdick, on cue.

'Yes, come along in a few minutes.' He had timed it perfectly. Audrey put down the receiver and, pointing towards the champagne in the bathroom, said, 'We are going to celebrate my engagement to Mr Fosdick.'

'So he's proposed to you?'

'Yes.'

'Where?'

'Does it matter?'

'Yes. Yes, it does.'

'Aliki, *please*.' Audrey's arms hung loosely at her sides and, seeing them there, fragile somehow and vulnerable, Aliki stepped towards her mother and reached out a hand. Audrey looked up, startled.

'Do you know that is the first time you have touched me voluntarily in years.'

'I know.' Aliki smiled. 'I hope you will be very happy.'

Audrey stood up and, peering into Aliki's face, said, 'There are times when you are very like your father.'

They smiled at each other as the knock came on the door,

and when they opened it and saw Mr Fosdick standing there, with a box of chocolates in one hand and a bunch of flowers in the other, the smiles broadened.

The ship was cutting smoothly into the dark sea by the time Captain Manoli and most of his three hundred guests were seated in the main lounge on Verandah Deck watching the farewell cabaret. It was later than usual for such activity, but the farewell dinner, with all its courses and the generous offering of free Greek wine, had absorbed the passengers in a way the captain had not meant. Some quirk of mind – possibly due to his attachment to the English generally – caused him to interfere with the night's menu, suggesting, then insisting, that dinner should be along the lines of an English Christmas dinner, although the menu would be as usual written out in French. The guests had been a little perplexed to find themselves confronted by a Dîner de Noël in the middle of a hot September night. The Dîner Rôti, Farceau Marrons and Sauce de Myrtilles had been all right, but the Pudding Anglais de Noël had sat heavily both on the plate and later in the stomach. But up on the dance floor, the passengers had begun to work it off, and humour was restored by the captain's game.

The captain smiled, patted his stomach and, turning to

the officer at the adjoining table, whispered something in his ear. At a nearby table Aliki saw the exchange between the officers, and it reminded her that in a few days they would be together in the same place with a new intake of passengers, the present batch entirely forgotten. She looked to her own table and to Audrey and Mr Fosdick sitting close together, his hand resting on the arm of her chair. She smiled as she thought of his perfect timing this evening and the conversation that had followed his arrival.

'Do you really think I can make her happy?' had been his opening question, and Aliki, startled, answered, 'Yes. I really think you can.' They had drunk the champagne, at first treating it as communion wine, the mood then altering to one of frivolity, and Mr Fosdick's long upper lip lifted back in an almost perpetual grin. It was only now, several courses of heavy food later, that a sort of sobriety was bringing Aliki back to her own question ... what about tomorrow?

On the dance floor, passengers were en bloc once more with the exception of Carl Roberts, who, with Elena held loosely in his arms, was demonstrating his nimble skill on the periphery of the floor. It didn't seem to matter that Peter Miller was now attached to Elena and was sitting here at the table with them, sharing the nightly bottle of champagne and enjoying the fancy dress that had been wished upon him.

'To you.' Peter Miller raised his glass and Aliki, deciding against the late-night abstinence she had promised herself, drank from the full glass that sat in front of her. 'I think you and Elena have done a great job on me,' he added, and his smile included those whose heads were still turned in his direction.

The competition to chose the man of the ship, 'Mr Laconia', had involved weightlifting, a display of strength generally, a recital of a national poem or song and then the invitation to dress up in drag. The captain had added this last challenge to settle an old score with the Englishman who, he guessed, would be chosen to represent his country.

'Drag!' Peter Miller protested.

Elena had led him out of the lounge, followed closely by Aliki. They had gone up the stairway to Carl's and Elena's stateroom where Aliki had discovered the various blonde wigs of this dark-haired Greek.

'That one.'

'No. That.'

'But this one suits his colouring.'

'Oh, all right then.'

Laughing and watching the transformation, Peter Miller stepped into a loose gown of shining silver as Elena applied the make-up.

Upstairs again, they watched as Captain Manoli looked from one contestant to another and pointed to the Major's large, hairy legs and feet. Feet that had marched the barrack square, climbed assault obstacles, gone over mountains, travelled on many a pheasant and grouse shoot had no place now under the exotic dress exposed to an Adriatic night. With the aid of shoe-horns and talcum powder, the other women had managed to get their men into shoes or slippers or sandals, and the men, with a self-conscious walk, which in fact gave credence to the character they were supposed to represent, simpered around the room, casting flirtatious looks towards the captain – the object of the game having been to see who, in the circumstances, could be the most seductive to him.

'Major Miller of England, fifth,' the captain concluded his judging, and Aliki, having watched carefully the look of satisfaction on Peter Miller's face, saw that the placing had confirmed his manliness. Now the Major sat in his drag clothes, displaying his defeat and smoking cigarettes through bright red lips, occasionally casting an eye towards the centre of the room where Daphne and Molly sat together in isolation. News had travelled fast about the Major's break with his wife and, shipboard life being what it is, sides had been taken. At first sympathy had been for Mrs Miller, as the Major represented the type of Englishman caricatured all too often. Now, in his present disguise, he confounded opinion.

Aliki sat on close to the Major, wondering about his future, about her own. She sipped at her glass and, staring at the bubbles still rising in it, tried to think what she would do if Costas had failed to give the note. What if the petty officer in charge had intercepted it before it had found its destination? What if Alexis was simply not interested?

Carl Roberts and Elena returned from the dance floor to drink more champagne, and as Carl offered the bottle around, Aliki leaned towards them and asked, 'What time does the

Verandah Bar close?' Together Carl and Elena answered, 'Midnight.'

Aliki looked at her watch. It was already one thirty, too late to ask Costas. She stood up, sat down again, looked round the lounge as if it had become a prison and jumped in her seat when Carl, putting his hand over hers, said, 'D'you care to dance?'

On the dance floor she found comfort in her partner's arms and in the joint rhythm of their movements. Everything, she felt suddenly, was going to be all right.

She said, 'If I ask you to do something for me, and it isn't difficult, will you do it without asking questions?'

'Ah'm too old a hand, honey, to fall for that one. Ah can't say if Ah will ask a question until Ah've heard what it is you want.'

'All right.' Aliki stopped at the side of the floor and, talking rapidly but quietly, said, 'If I get my steward to deliver my luggage to your stateroom first thing in the morning would you be prepared to take it with you to …?' She looked at him.

'To the Danieli,' he suggested. He was smiling his crooked grin, and she, feeling that he had guessed she was deceiving Audrey, wondered if he saw himself as the white knight to the rescue.

She'd noticed that he had made no attempt during the cruise to penetrate Audrey's decorative exterior, showing for it an almost open dislike. Now perhaps he saw himself as the means whereby Aliki could manoeuvre her freedom.

'Anything Ah can do to help will be a pleasure,' he said, 'but remember, Ah'm not having any part in arrangements you may be making with this deck-phantom, this death-partner.'

'Carl!' She moved very close to him. 'There *is* a man I meet on deck.'

He stood his ground as the couples circled. 'Are you taking this crazy idea with you when we dock tomorrow?'

'When the ship docks in Venice I am going ashore with him, and I want to be free of most of my luggage.'

He put his hands on her shoulders, his face solemn at last. 'If you have your luggage delivered to my cabin you will come ashore with me.'

'And Elena? What about her?'

He enfolded her once more in his large and supportive arms and joined the dancers.

With the urgency gone out of the moment and with a feeling of relief that this large American had her in support, Aliki looked round the lounge and felt a strange affection for the individuals among the sea of faces. They were no longer a blurred crowd scene at the back of a painting. These were the faces attached to the personalities that had stepped out of the canvas. She smiled at them all, and Carl Roberts, believing that the smile was for him, lent forward and kissed her lightly on the lips. 'Think about coming with me,' he said again, and she, seeing the benign, kindly expression on his face and deciding suddenly not to play either the innocent or the coquette, said, 'Yes. Yes, I will.'

They held hands as they returned to the table, and Peter Miller, standing up to bow Aliki back to her seat, drew many glances at the sight of this drag queen behaving with all the air of an English gentleman.

Voices sank lower, and the gentle sounds from the piano in the corner seemed to ease out the departing guests.

Aliki kept time to the music, her fingers gently drumming on the table. Soon she would have to face the possible consequence of her note to Alexis. She sank bank into her chair. If she stayed where she was, talking to the stewards as they tidied the lounge, she could turn her back on the strange world that had been created for her – or which she had created – down in cabin A29. If she stayed on well into disembarkation, she would never have to know if Alexis had or had not responded to her letter.

'… I think that's about it.'

She looked up, startled, to see the Major in Elena's dress hovering above. Around them the room was empty. 'There's no point in going back to my cabin,' he said. 'What about a walk round the deck?'

She stood up and, putting an arm through the chiffon one beside her, said, 'Yes. A walk round the deck is just what I need.'

Together they walked, and the two figures that came out of the wall-mirror towards them were smiling with a combination of amusement and anticipation.

'Neither of us,' Aliki said, speaking towards the glass, 'has the least idea of what tomorrow may bring.'

Sunlight was well into the cabin by the time Aliki was in the shower the next morning. Rubbing oil over herself, she sang as she sprayed cold water on to her head and down her body. To a knock at the door she called out, 'Come in.'

She sang on, her voice high but tuneless, and, coming out from behind the shower curtain wrapped in a towel, she grinned broadly at her steward, who was standing staring at the empty cabin.

'Is good you tell me what you do with luggage.' His eyes were wide and his expression solemn.

Aliki wanted to kiss him and tell him it was none of his business, and that soon he would be worrying about another passenger, and that ... But she could see that he was hurt and deflated, as if the joy of the anticipated farewell had been removed. Besides, he was suspicious, and she said, 'I asked the night steward to remove the luggage.' Her plans did not include Nikos. She could not trust him, even at this last moment of the cruise, not to take matters into his own hands.

'Removed where to?' He stood stiffly in front of her, and the sweet-sour smell of him filled the emptiness of the room.

'Actually, Nikos, to the luggage hold.'

Nikos took the yellow duster out of his jacket pocket and flicked it across the dressing-table. 'You tell me!'

'Yes, I tell you.' Anger flushed her face. 'It is not your business what I do with my luggage.'

'Is not coming, your man.'

'Which man?'

'He you meet on deck.'

The knock that came on the open door startled them both. They turned together and, whereas Nikos saw a crew member from the engine-room, Aliki saw a small stranger, behind whom stood a ship's officer.

The officer nodded to the crew member, who said, 'I am Stavros Zervudachi. You sent for me.'

She looked from the crew member to the officer, and from the officer to Nikos. The crew member stood motionless, his face a blank.

She turned to Nikos. 'Do you know this man?'

'I know him.' Nikos also stood motionless.

She studied the squat stranger, laughter beginning to choke in her throat. Laughter and disbelief, followed by – was it? – relief. 'I'm sorry,' she managed. 'There has been a mistake.'

Stavros Zervudachi eyed her up and down. Then, shrugging his shoulders, he turned on his heels, waited for the officer and went through the door.

She swung round, laughing fully. 'And you'd better go too,' she said to Nikos. 'And take the whole mystique of this cabin with you.'

'Please.' Nikos held out a hand. 'What you say?'

The look of hurt dismay reached her. 'Nothing, Nikos. It's just that ...' She reached for her bag and took out the money set aside for him and his family.

'For your wife and children,' she said, and Nikos, the true

Greek that he was, smiled a broad, forgiving, black-toothed grin, looked the lady in the face and said, 'Is my honour to look after you.'

She held both his hands in hers. 'Thanks. For everything.'

At the door he pivoted. 'Is good you go with Mr Roberts.'

He went quickly through the door and she, calling after him, said, 'You think so, do you? Well, if *you* think so, then that's what I'd better do.'

Hurriedly now, as if fate might intervene, she threw on her clothes and, reaching into the dressing-table drawer, pulled out a sheet of writing paper.

'Carl,' she wrote, 'I'm leaving the ship alone, and taking the slow way back to London. I don't want to be lumbered with my luggage so the night steward is bringing it to your stateroom.' She added a P.S: 'You're right, he was a phantom.'

Taking a last look round the cabin, she looked up to the fresco now static on the wall. She studied it for a last time and saw that it was of Minoan figures walking through beautiful gardens as they conducted their dead into funerary palaces. 'Thank you,' she said. 'And goodbye.'

She zipped up the small hold-all on the bed and, flinging it over her shoulder, stepped through the door and went quickly down the passageway.

Captain Manoli stood on the bridge, observing final disembarkation. He had been at the exit on A Deck to see off and say goodbye to most of the passengers. Good host that he was, he had said to each, 'We shall hope to see you again.' Some, he knew, would be back; others, such as the German professor and his wife, would never again afford it. The professor had thanked him for everything done for them by the ship's company, and in his thanks he had included the good services of the doctor. Doctor Anagnosti had come up to see Mrs McAllister walk slowly off the ship with her daughter, and both he and the captain had been amused and touched to see the crippled German offer to help the invalid down the gangway. The captain had watched the German couple take leave of the English group to which they had become attached, and was pleased and relieved to see that handshakes from other passengers for Mrs Miller and Mrs Wainwright were as warm as for anyone else. The Major had come walking off the ship alone, but his head held high, because, as he told the captain, he was to be taken round the bright spots of Venice by the ever-engaging Elena. The captain had missed a personal goodbye with Mrs Martin and Aliki Findlay because, just as Mrs Martin and – it now seemed a fixture – Mr Fosdick were going through, the vociferous Salvi family from Napoli had appeared and engulfed him in a multiple embrace. He had more or less guessed what Mrs Findlay was up to, because the night steward of A Deck had done his duty in reporting to the head steward where the lady's luggage had gone. Now, casting a final glance at the farewell gestures on the quay, he turned to the last and most influential of his passengers, waiting for him up on the bridge wing.

'Ah should say it has been a most successful cruise.' Carl Roberts smiled at the captain, and, leaning a little further over the rail, added, 'Elena is taking the Major in hand. She is all sunshine, that woman.' He laughed, the crooked grin going well up the side of his face, and, turning back to the captain, said, 'As you know, Ah've been telephoning mah office every day because Ah was most anxious to get the affair settled before we docked in Venice.'

Captain Manoli, standing stiffly now, in the manner he adopted for hastening farewells, was in fact torn between wishing to take hold of the broad hand to hasten departure and prolonging the goodbye in favour of another visit from this pleasing American.

'... So you see,' Carl Roberts was saying, 'it'll only really be a matter of a couple of signatures before...'

'What signatures?' the captain asked abruptly, and, seeing the broad hand gripped possessively on the ship's rail, looked into the smiling acquisitive face and understood at last that Mr Roberts and his company had been extending their shopping list.

'Yes, sir,' he said respectfully, but without any subservience.

Carl Roberts's shout reached Aliki as she sped across the quay. She turned, looked up and blew him a kiss.

'You'll see her again,' Carl Roberts observed, and Captain Manoli, who was trying to equate the dynamic-looking woman departing there with the pale lady of the start of the cruise, smiled and said, 'Shall we?'

'Yeah. But next time without the mother.'

Carl Roberts patted the captain on the shoulder and, thinking of the letter that had just been slipped under his door, said to himself, 'If she's out there savouring freedom, I'll take my time about getting her bags back to her in London.' He grinned, laughed a little. He was going to have some fun with the future.